Emile de Laveleye

Luxury

Emile de Laveleye

Luxury

ISBN/EAN: 9783337304034

Printed in Europe, USA, Canada, Australia, Japan

Cover: Foto ©Andreas Hilbeck / pixelio.de

More available books at **www.hansebooks.com**

BY

EMILE DE LAVELEYE.

Professor of Political Economy in the University of Liège, Member of the
Belgian Royal Academy, Correspondent of the French Institute and
of the Royal Academies of Madrid, Lisbon, Rome, &c.,
and Honorary D.C.L. of Edinburgh and
Würzburg Universities.

SECOND   EDITION

LONDON:

SWAN SONNENSCHEIN & CO..

1891.

TABLE OF CONTENTS.

LAW AND MORALS IN POLITICAL ECONOMY.

LUXURY.

———•———

CHAPTER I.

THE QUESTION AT ISSUE.

IN the 18th century people held long and lively discussions on the subject of Luxury. To-day we do not discuss it so frequently; we are content with indulging in it to excess.

Is luxury useful? This is the question we need to decide. I have read somewhere, no matter where, a saying which seems to me exactly to sum up the discussion. A financier and an economist of the last century held entirely different opinions on this subject.

A

"I maintain, for my part," said the financier, "that it is luxury which upholds States." "Yes," replied the economist, "just as the executioner's rope upholds the hanged man." I agree with the economist. The philosophers of old times and the fathers of the Church alike condemned luxury in the strongest terms, and they were right in so doing. It is pernicious to the individual, and fatal to society. Primitive Christianity reproved it in the name of charity and of humility; political economy condemns it in the name of utility, and right in the name of equity.

CHAPTER II.

WHAT IS LUXURY?

FIRST let us make it plain what we understand by luxury. M. Baudrillart, in his excellent book, "Histoire du luxe," does not trouble to seek a definition. He takes for granted that every one knows what it means. I do not quarrel with him for this, but we shall be none the worse for a little precision.

I understand by a luxury anything which does not answer to our primary needs, and which, since it costs much money to buy, and consequently much labour to produce, is only within reach of the few. The extreme of luxury is that which destroys the

3

product of many days of labour without bringing any rational satisfaction to the owner. The queen of the ball-room destroys in the mazes of the waltz a lace skirt worth 10,000 francs: there you have the equivalent of 50,000 hours of labour, and labour of the most tedious kind, and fatal to the eyes, destroyed in a moment. And what advantage has anyone derived from it? M. de Keratry defines luxury as "that which creates imaginary needs, exaggerates real wants, diverts them from their true end, establishes a habit of prodigality in society, and offers through the senses a satisfaction of self-love which puffs up, but does not nourish, the heart, and which presents to others the picture of a happiness to which they can never attain."

The very definition of luxury which to me seems the best contains in it the condemnation of luxury. It follows from it that a thing may be an object of luxury at one period, and may cease to be so at another, when it can be procured without great expense. As

Roscher says, in his chapters on this subject ("Principles of Political Economy "), luxury is entirely *relative*.

Every nation and every age considers everything as superfluous which they do not habitually use. Holinshed, in his chronicle, groans over the ultra-refinement of the English in his times (1577), because they were everywhere introducing chimneys, instead of allowing the smoke to escape through cracks in the roof, and were using vessels of earthenware, or even of tin, in place of the old wooden bowls and jugs. Another author of the same period, Slaney, " On Rural Expenditure," is indignant that oak should be used in building, instead of willow. " Formerly," he exclaims, " houses were of willow and men were of oak ; now-a-days, houses are of oak and men are of willow." In the Middle Ages linen was so rare that princesses would make a present of a shirt to their betrothed, and it was the general custom in going to bed to take off even this first garment. It would be considered to-day the very extreme of misery to be reduced to dispensing with this. When flowered cottons and muslins first were introduced from India, wealthy ladies only could wear them; now, working-men's wives despise them. Thus the progress of mechanical skill brings by degrees more and more objects within reach of the majority. But the above definition remains true: everything is a luxury which is at the same time dear and superfluous.

CHAPTER III.

SENTIMENTS WHICH GIVE RISE TO LUXURY.

M. BAUDRILLART, in his book already quoted, gives a fine and searching analysis of the various sentiments in man which give rise to luxury. He distinguishes three, which he finds to be natural and universal, vanity, sensuality, and the instinct of adornment.

First, vanity : the wish to distinguish one's self and to appear of more importance than others. Since wealth and power win the admiration of the crowd, one is happy when one is considered rich and powerful. Here is a necklace of valuable pearls : a woman will pay £4,000 for it. Is it for the sake of possessing a beautiful thing, or does she hope to beautify herself

7

by wearing it? No, for artificial pearls are more regular and have as much brilliancy. But a necklace which cost an immense amount of money will be the sign and symbol of her wealth. Those who see it will say, "She is rich," and her rivals, who are not so rich as herself, will be jealous, which will season the sauce of her vanity. People seek satisfaction, and, so to speak, a factitious existence, in the opinion of others. This is a very general sentiment and wonderfully powerful.

When public opinion bows only before virtue, vanity or self-love becomes a powerful stimulus for good. When, on the contrary, public opinion worships wealth, this sentiment urges men to luxury and corruption.

Vanity, and the love of fine clothes which it engenders, are very marked among the savages who tattoo themselves before putting on garments; and they become more refined in civilised man, in what is called society. But a high state of culture and the growing empire of reason temper them and give them a less evil direction. Formerly, men as well as women wore brilliant stuffs, ribbons, laces, and jewels, and it is still the custom in China and among savage peoples. But, since the beginning of this century, civilised nations have borrowed from England the black suit of the quaker. For a man to wear diamonds, even as shirt buttons, is considered very bad taste. Simplicity, extreme neatness, and cleanliness constitute the whole of masculine elegance.

Women, on the other hand, still love to pierce their ears to hang from them certain stones, or to surround their neck with beads or small pieces of metal, as in the Isles of the Pacific, or in the days of pre-historic man. Every year they seek some new mode of rendering their garments more inconvenient and more costly. How shall we set about curing this infirmity, this relic of primitive barbarism? Stuart Mill tells us in his book on the condition of woman: Give her such instruction as will set her at work on the matters of mind, and, like the modern man, she will cease to find pleasure in feathers and finery. A chimera, do you say? Feminine vanity is an incurable evil? I do not believe a word of it. Christianity wrought this miracle among the Quakers, and in the monasteries; why should it not be wrought to-day by the sense of justice allied to the culture of reason?

The time is not so far distant since Buckingham, at the Court of France, wore in his costume such quantities of diamonds that he could scatter them on the floor and see the queen's ladies-in-waiting on their knees picking them up. If the black dress-coat has taken the place of the silken garments and trimmings of lace, why should not a similar change be wrought in the costume of women? Throughout the whole period of classical antiquity, were they not content with the linen tunic and the chlamys of fine wool?

As luxury in this instance has its root in vanity, what we need is to change the current of opinion. If public opinion were sufficiently enlightened to understand that luxury is a thing barbarous, infantine, immoral, and, above all, *wrong,* the woman, who to-day dresses herself in costly clothes in order to please and to be imposing, would content herself with being beautiful or pretty at a slight cost, which is certainly the most charming fashion of so being.

Among the orators of the pulpit we find the most eloquent condemnations of the luxury which is the result of vanity. Bossuet is admirable on this subject. "Look at that woman in her superb beauty, in her ostentation, in her grand array. She desires to conquer, to be adored as a goddess in human form, but she adores herself first of all; herself is her own idol." And again: "Men make a display of their daughters; they render them a spectacle of vanity and the objects of public cupidity.

They foster in this way their vanity and that of others." And, finally, in a terribly powerful passage: "This woman," he cries, "ambitious and vain thinks to enhance her own value by loading herself with gold, with precious stones, and a thousand other adornments. In order to deck her in braver array the whole nation exhausts itself; the arts groan and sweat in the laborious service; the whole range of industry wears itself out."

This kind of luxury then, springing from ostentation, needs only that its childish folly and emptiness be universally demonstrated in order for its extirpation.

But the second kind, that, namely, which has its root in the cravings of sensuality, is far more difficult to contend with, inasmuch as this does at least afford some satisfaction and enjoyment, very superficial no doubt, but, nevertheless, real. On this subject M. Baudrillart has some very just reflections to offer. "Matter is in its nature finite, and sensuality, like it, has also its limits. But man cherishes the illusion that this is not so. It seems to him that he has never sucked out all the sweets of enjoyment; and when he has exhausted one form of pleasure, he runs after another. Every refinement of delight admits of still further refining, and another must always be ready when the last has ceased to charm. Here again, how many factitious wants are satisfied which never had any existence, save in the imagination! What priceless value comes to be attached to shades of difference indiscoverable by any but experts. In the same way self-love establishes a superiority in the veriest trifles, and there are delicacies distinguished by marks which are not patent to the senses of the vulgar. The heavy price paid for such things enhances the enjoyment of them, since it adds to their intrinsic charm the piquancy of a difficulty overcome."

Vanity exalts sensuality, but very often serves it to no good purpose. The extreme of refinement and of abundance alike engender satiety. Nowadays our menus are so crowded that the tables of kings can find nothing to add to them, and all varieties of wine circulate in succession, so that soon the jaded palate ceases to distinguish one taste from another, and the guest eats at random. How much more savoury, how much more charming, were once those little dinners, so well depicted by Brillat Savarin, where they made merry over some fine, old, home-made wine, some choice dish carefully prepared, a masterpiece of culinary art, which was appreciated at its full value by the unspoilt appetite of the guests. They tasted everything with a shade of compunction, and at dessert came outbursts of frank laughter, merry jokes and songs. Whither is it departed, the sparkling gaiety of our fathers? Luxury and the pursuit of millions have destroyed it altogether.

Man has one stomach, and one only. When all is said, his needs are but limited. It is possible without excessive spending to afford the senses all real satisfaction, and a man who aims at real comfort will not be ruined. What costs so much is *ostentation*, the desire to shine. To this, in fact, there is no limit. When Cleopatra swallowed a pearl which had been dissolved in her golden chalice, when Heliogabalus devoured a plateful of nightingales' tongues, was it from sensuality ? . . . . . .

Abundance of all that is useful may be assured to us by the progress made in the art of production, but when once men are fired with the ambition to distinguish themselves, it becomes a question of the lavish use of all that is most costly and rare; and hence of the destruction in a moment of the result of long and arduous labour. Herein lies the very essence of luxury, and herein also its inhuman perversity. Let us hope that good sense will at long last correct and regulate even this species of dementia.

M. Baudrillart, as we have seen, traces a third source of luxury, the instinct of adornment. He says very truly, "This instinct is to be distinguished from ostentation even when it closely borders on it, and from sensuality which it may sometimes subserve." This instinct it is which gives birth to decorative and industrial art. It is a very primitive human instinct; even the pre-historic races who lived in caves during the glacial period have left engraved on fragments of bone, drawings of the reindeer and the beaver, which in those days inhabited these lands. Being constantly cultivated and refined it grows into the æsthetic sense, that love of the beautiful which has created all the arts—architecture, sculpture, painting, and the art of the potter. Far from condemning it, we should seek to uphold and elevate it, for in our public monuments it becomes an agent of civilisation and a source of pure disinterested enjoyment which is accessible at all times, and to the whole nation. Applied in private life to the decoration of dwellings, to furniture, utensils, and in everything to the choice of beautiful forms, as in the days of classic antiquity, it purifies taste and becomes thus an instrument of progress.

Animals, even, are attracted by brilliancy of colour, and perhaps, also, by the beauty of lines.[1] Naturalists find in this one of the principal causes of the perfecting of species.

The love of beauty, therefore, in itself would work for the amelioration of the human species, if it were not so often checked by the love of riches. Suppress the dowry, or establish equality of conditions, and your strong, handsome youth will marry a beautiful

[1] Thus there is in Australia a bird, the Chlamyderis, called in the English colonies the bower-bird, which makes little gardens in front of its nest, adorned with shells and bright-coloured flowers. Again, in the grotto of Spy in Belgium, once inhabited by primitive men with flattened skulls, objects have been found engraved with markings which form the rudiments of decoration.

B

and graceful girl: from their union will come generations of vigorous and healthy men and women.   In
these days a misshapen dwarf or a wretched hunch-
back, armed with their millions, will find a mate, and
will transmit to their descendants their own defects
of character and form.   Thus the race is ruined by
extreme inequality of conditions.

The love of the beautiful and the instinct of adornment are things good in themselves, and they do not
necessarily encourage luxury, since they take delight,
if they are pure, not in the costliness of the material,
but in the harmony of the colouring and in the purity
of the lines.   A gold or silver statue covered with
jewels is revolting to good taste.   The figures of this
kind which are to be seen in Catholic churches
are horrible.   But what can be more charming than
these little terra-cotta statuettes of Tanagra, made
from materials that cost less than a halfpenny!   It is
to periods of decay in art that the poet's words apply:

"Materiam superabat opus," and that the remark could be made to a Greek sculptor, "You have made Venus rich because you could not make her beautiful."

M. Baudrillart brings out very skilfully the difference which there is between luxury and art. "Art has for its aim the realisation of the ideal of beauty, or, again, the reproduction of certain forms. Luxury has but one object: to make a display. The object of art is essentially disinterested; that of luxury essentially selfish. The beautiful itself, which is the goal passionately sought by the true artist, always longing for perfection, what does it mean to the devotee of luxury? Nothing but what glitters. The luxurious pay for art by the yard and by the pound: they buy its masterpieces as they lavish money on jewels and stuffs."

M. Baudrillart names lastly, as an additional source of luxury, the desire for change. This for the most part expresses itself in the caprices of fashion, and is, in fact, the scourge of our time. In former days each country had its own mode of dress, generally dictated by the necessities of climate or of local production. These national costumes, picturesque, solid, and durable, were transmitted from generation to generation. Now-a-days society everywhere has the same general style of dress, but the fashions, especially among women, change every spring. A famous dressmaker invents a new cut, and from Paris to Shanghai, from London to San-Francisco, everyone will adopt it, discarding the costumes of the previous year. There are many different evils traceable entirely to these fluctuations of fashion. M. Baudrillart illustrates them by some apt quotations.

First, they engender frivolity, and distract the mind from matters with which it ought to be occupied. "Those who pride themselves on being elegant are obliged to occupy a considerable portion of their time with their clothes, and to study them in a way which assuredly does not tend to elevate the mind or to render it capable of great things." This is the moral evil.

The economic evil is well described by J. B. Say: "Fashion is privileged to consider things useless which have not yet come to be so, things, often, which have not even lost their first freshness: fashion multiplies consumption, and condemns what is still in excellent condition, convenient, it may be pretty, to be no longer good for anything. Thus the rapid changes of fashion impoverish a state both by what they consume and by what they do not consume."

For the manufacture of any new designs in silk, wool, or cotton, there are first expenses in the way of models, cartoons, printing rollers, and I know not what besides. All that does not sell in the same year becomes sale-stock to be cleared off at low prices; some goods are not fancied, remain unsold, and go at last at half-price. All these outlays and all these losses must, at last, be covered by the proceeds of sale, or the manufacturer will be ruined and will cease to produce. The changes of fashion thus considerably increase the price of all articles which are subject to them.

Suppose we had, as formerly, an unvarying national costume: the current manufacture of material it would require could be done at much less cost than that of the thousands of different styles which every year break out in the spring and winter fashions. The Queen of Roumania is trying to induce the ladies of her country to adopt the delightful costume of the Wallachian peasantry, and she herself is setting them the example.

" What !" you will say ; "you wish to condemn us to a stupifying monotony, and to deprive us of the piquancy of novelty !" Do you then believe that the best use mankind can make of capital, science and taste, is to place them at the services of the purveyors of fashions ? Have women nothing better to do than to invent new combinations for their toilette, to talk incessantly about dress and fashion, and to envy each other the possession of such things ?

It is possible to conceive of garments suited to the seasons of the year which would combine in a high degree comfort and elegance. Material, cut, and colours would all be decided on æsthetic lines and on hygienic principles. This once done, it should be everywhere kept to.

In England a society of ladies has been formed to forward the introduction of rational dress.

But already I hear it said, " Good heavens ! why not give us at once the gown of the Carmelite or the robe of the Capuchin ? " I reply first that it was a profound and far-reaching idea which imposed on the religious orders a costume which has remained un-changed for eighteen centuries. It is a means by which the human soul is withdrawn, at least on one side, from the region of those futilities in which vanity takes delight, that it may be the more free to rise towards the level of things eternal. Further, let us not forget that from the most ancient Greek vases down to the frescoes in catacombs of the third and fourth centuries, ancient art presents to us figures all clad in the same manner.

Leisure and studied elegance induce frivolity, and from this spring the caprices of fashion. When laws shall be more just, and men's souls more noble, and their brains better supplied with good sense, then we shall at length come to do as did the ancients.

CHAPTER IV.

LUXURY IS UNJUSTIFIABLE.

HAVING analysed the various sentiments of the human heart which give rise to luxury, we pass on to consider in what light we ought to regard it. Many authors, and among them M. Baudrillart, take up an intermediate position between the austere school, which preaches the retrenchment of needs, and the laxer school, which considers luxury as a thing agreeable to the individual and necessary for the State, making a distinction between luxury which is honest, permissible, praiseworthy even, and luxury which is improper and immoral. I, for my part, do not admit this distinction, and I believe that the

25

austere school were altogether right. Those condemnations of luxury which, with so much unanimity
and so much eloquence, have been pronounced alike
by the philosophers and sages of antiquity, and by
the fathers of the Church, and the orators of the
Christian pulpit, are completely justified by the re-
searches of modern science. They were ignorant of
political economy, but they were inspired by the
instinct of justice and of right, and, after the
Christian era, by the idea of charity and of human
brotherhood.

All that is really luxury cannot be other than
immoral, unjust, and inhuman. Let us hear what
one of the fathers of political economy has to say on
this: "Those persons," said J. B. Say, "who by means
of great talents or the possession of great power seek
to spread the taste for luxury are guilty of conspir-
ing against the well-being of nations."

Luxury consists, as we have seen, in the consumption of what has cost great labour to produce, for the satisfaction of spurious needs. When labour is so necessary to procure for mankind the satisfaction of legitimate needs, when so many human beings still live in almost entire destitution, can it be good or even legitimate to use a large proportion of the forces placed at our disposal by capital and labour for the production of superfluities which, indeed, in many cases, we had better be without ?

In order to emphasise clearly the point wherein I venture to differ from M. Baudrillart, I will take one of his own examples, that of diamonds. M. Blanqui, writing of the Kohinoor or "Mountain of Light," had said : "Diamonds have always seemed to me very foolish and useless things, although women always covet them as the chiefest of ornaments." M. Baudrillart replies that for the year 1878, to say nothing of the ten preceding years, diamonds found represented a value of 350 millions, that more than 20,000 workmen are employed in getting them out of mines, and more than 3000 lapidaries of Holland, Belgium, and France in cutting them, and that these earn good salaries, half-a-crown for the apprentices, and the master lapidaries from 12s. to 16s. "Is all this," he asks, finally, "of no use at all?"

It is my opinion that a thing may be valued at enormous sums, and be, not only quite useless, but very harmful. The Chinese buy from the English £16,000,000 worth of opium; this is worse than useless. It is a poison, and the Emperor of China would do well to fling into the sea all the cases of this abominable narcotic which England palms off upon him. These are what I call false riches. To maintain that wealth consists of labour is, as Bastiat says, nothing but a *sisyphism*, or making work for work's sake. I see thousands of workers, it is true, at work in the mines or in the shops, and receiving good salaries. But if the diamonds which they are finding, or cutting, have no other effect than to excite bad feeling, to arouse vanity in those that possess them, and envy in those who cannot, would it not be better to seek the ocean-bed for these precious stones, in company with the opium? If these same workers were employed in making shirts, and shoes, and stockings for those who have none, would there not be better cause for congratulation? For my own part, I would rather see fifty women each wearing a dress that cost a pound than one wearing a ball-dress which cost £400.

I am not calling for sumptuary laws, but I rejoice when I see a country like Norway, and the mountain Cantons of Switzerland, where no one buys diamonds, but everyone has sufficient means to procure the necessaries of life.

The main point, and the one which is most often forgotten, is this: every article of luxury costs much labour—could not this labour be utilized in a more rational fashion ? If we take the case of an isolated individual, we shall see more clearly the point of this.

Would any man be insane enough to devote three years of his existence to making himself a piece of jewelry which in point of fact will be of no real use to him ? It is the phenomena of exchange which hide from us the absurdity of it, the fact that he who wears it has ordered it from some one else. But when we consider the whole of humanity as one being, obliged to satisfy his wants by his labour, we can see clearly that it is folly for him to waste precious time in cutting diamonds, if he still has often to walk with bare feet. The inhabitants of any country have but a certain limited number of hours in the day to dispose of; if they devote half this time to making useless trifles, it is inevitable that half the population should go without the necessaries of life. An Emperor of China once said : "If one of my subjects is idle and does not work then there is somewhere in my State another who suffers from hunger and cold." To dig a hole and fill it up again, to embroider shirt-fronts, or set precious stones, is not really to work, for it is not productive of the least utility.

My quarrel with M. Baudrillart is not for being too indulgent towards what he calls "mischievous luxury"; it is for admitting that there can be luxury which is not mischievous. Luxury, to my thinking, cannot be other than mischievous. The very word, it seems to me, implies an idea of blame. When he deals with "mischievous luxury," M. Baudrillart attacks it eloquently and with energy. Let us hear him: "Men were right in regarding as an axiom the proposition: *luxury is enervating.* They were not less right in adding: *and it corrupts.* It destroys the manly energy of the mind by cultivating a taste for mere enjoyment, and a pride in mere frivolity. It kills the spirit of self-sacrifice, without which no society can continue to exist; it undermines at once the power of any lively impulse towards good, and of any determined resistance of evil. Men live for the sake of pleasure; public spirit ceases to have any motive power. Historians and moralists are unanimous in pointing out the inevitable decay which follows on the worship of ease and refinement, and the debasement of character which this produces. More than ever, in our days, the mere owner of wealth, idle and dissipated, seems a shocking anomaly. We are finding it hard to accept the idea of rights without duties. Luxury then brings moral discredit on ownership, dissipating in frivolity and wrong-doing."

In another fine passage, M. Baudrillart sums up Rousseau's diatribe against towns, though, he adds, that in this matter we must not forget what statistics show as to the advantages they procure and the virtues they develop. "Towns are hot-beds of luxury and corruption! It is there that men's wants are over-excited by a thousand stimulants, it is there that are crowded together all those species of delights which do not wait upon desire but call it forth. There all the vanities and all the vices spread in contagious competition. The art of frivolity settles on the ruins of the useful arts, nay, the very necessary arts which serve the needs of all are choked out of existence by this flux of superfluities which are serviceable only to the few. Every moment the revolting contrast strikes one between excessive opulence and extreme misery —rags, tatters, and even nakedness, on the one hand, and on the other the flaunting array of all the trappings of opulence. Here, splendid dwellings; there, a hearth without a fire; here, vice, elegant and gay; there, vice in its most brutal form, the crime of those who seek both vengeance on, and a participation in this wealth which crushes them down. For them there is temptation everywhere; shops by thousands, filled with all that the poor lack, displaying stores of gold, jewels, and fine costumes. Out of this state of things spring hatred and envy in the hearts of the poor, raging there in secret, only to break out from time to time in those tumults in which he who has nothing seeks to enforce a claim to his share of enjoyment." What more could be said even by the most fervent disciple of the austere school, whom, nevertheless, M. Baudrillart taxes with extravagance? But the point of difference is that he regards a certain degree of luxury—a moderate, and not immoral degree, of course—as an indispensable stimulus to work which would not be found in the supply of necessary wants alone. In this I cannot agree with him, and I will proceed to give my reasons.

I admit with Stuart Mill that, in order to arouse those races which are still in the savage state from the sort of animal inertia and dull stagnation in which they live, it may be good to excite in them new wants which will make them work and contrive in order to satisfy them. But among the nations of Europe it is not the desire for consumption which needs stimulating. "Nay, but see," says M. Baudrillart, "the wretched creatures crowded into the cellars of Lille, the doss-houses of London. They are happy in their dirt and darkness, and have no desire to come out of it." I ask, Is this reproach well-founded? These unfortunate creatures work, nevertheless; they toil and suffer to earn subsistence. Can we reproach them with the fact that what they can earn is so insufficient that it drives them into holes and corners where a farmer would not house his dogs or even his pigs? The very large majority of even a rich nation like the French has not the lodging, furniture, raiment, or food, which hygiene prescribes, and they all most certainly wish for it. Is it possible that this desire for the necessaries of life would not be strong enough to stimulate men to work? It is the only stimulus of those who perform manual labour, and it is precisely the idle who seek for superfluities.

"But what will you do, wiseacres," cries M. Baudrillart, "with the thousands of artists and hundreds of thousands of workmen who work in metals, stuffs, ivory, wood, or gems, executing products of infinite taste?" Yet, some pages further on, the eminent economist himself answers this question, in refuting the argument of those who maintain that "France produces too much." "In what respect does she produce too much, this happy country of ours? It is not in respect of the whole sum of useful and pleasant things in life—for there are too many poor! Show me, if you can, the article which is produced in superabundance. Is it flannel, when so many are cold? Is it corn, when so many lack bread?"

Here lies the solution of the problem: those workmen who work in ivory and in gems should produce the flannel and the corn which you say are so much wanted now, and the problem would be solved. The same amount of work, but of a more useful kind.

"But you cannot distinguish," our author goes on to urge, " between the superfluous which you mean to proscribe and the necessary you wish to multiply." It is true the idea of luxury is relative and depends on the means of production : what is superfluous to-day will be no longer so to-morrow, if the progress of the mechanical arts have placed it within reach of all. Yet, for all that, I hold that the distinction is always easy to make : is an object worth the pain it would require and the time it would take for me to make it myself ? If so, it is not a luxury, and I am right in securing it ; but if, in obtaining it, I divert human effort from a channel in which it would be more useful, I am wrong. I sacrifice things necessary to things superfluous. I am making a bad use of my own or my fellow-creatures' powers.

CHAPTER V.

IS LUXURY ANY EVIDENCE OR CAUSE OF MORAL DEVELOPMENT?

M. BAUDRILLART gives the following title to one of his paragraphs: "Limited and scanty range of wants a sign of inferiority. Material needs as related to moral development." This is true of the dawn of civilisation: later on it is true no longer. Under the stimulus of want, man betakes himself to labour, with coarse and clumsy implements at first—a rough flint, a stake hardened in the fire, the skeletons of fish, or a fragment of bone sharpened at the point—then by degrees with more and more elaborated instruments of metal. As Ludwig Noiré brings out so well in his excellent book *Das Werkzeng* (Tools), in the course of manufacturing implements, the human creature manufactures also languages, and grows rapidly into a higher degree of intelligence. Soon he learns to co-ordinate and arrange his observations of natural forces. Technical skill and science next come into the field. Social relations are established, and the rude manners of the savage are softened. Agriculture makes it to the interest of all who take it up to maintain peace and good order. Man is no longer a mere carnivorous animal, whose whole time is spent in hunting prey, devouring and digesting it. The leisure which he secures as the result of the greater productivity of work opens to him the vast horizon of intellectual and moral life.

As M. Baudrillart aptly expresses it, "In learning to modify the things he sees around him, the man is accomplishing his own education. They are not more transformed than he is himself, when, of his own accord, he sets himself to work on them with thoughtful effort. His labour creates for him a new world. We may even say, it makes a new man of him; in fine, it makes all that we mean by *man.* Work brings forth new faculties. Work demands prudence and forethought; it pre-supposes a knowledge of the relation of means to ends. Is this all? No; it means also the establishment of relations with other men, relations necessarily of a reciprocal kind; it means the first beginnings of social life, properly so called. And this social life will go on spreading, little by little, to the ends of the earth, through the interchange of services and of products of all kinds."

This fine panegyric of labour is completely justified so long as it is applied to the production of necessaries. When it is devoted to the creation of useless trifles, it is a culpable waste of time, which is the stuff our lives are made of, and is given us for higher ends; it is so much stolen from the training of the mind, and from the cultivation of domestic and social relations.

So far from the extreme development of wants being a sign of the progress of civilisation, it is in times of laxity, corruption and decay that wants become most numerous, and are carried to an extreme of refinement. The Roman Empire serves as example and proof of this. Roscher speaks well on this point. There we see men occupied in the pursuit of the impossible, and their ideal of luxury is to find the highest pleasure in what is most perverse. As Seneca says of Caligula: "Nihil tam efficere concupiscebat quam quod posse effici negaretur. Hoc est luxuriæ propositum gaudere perversis." Men thus do violence to nature. Such an Emperor will join Baiae to Pucciola by a bridge across the sea, solely that he may pass along it in his triumphal car. Such another will have mountains levelled or raised. Æsop, the comedian, places before his guests a dish consisting of the tongues of parrots which had learned to speak; this represented a cost of £56,000. Hortensius would water his trees with wine. I need go no further; the insane vagaries of the thirst of enjoyment are well known to us all. I say then, have we here any connection between the development of wants and moral progress?

It is the habit of economists, I know, and of the general current of opinion also, to measure the degree of civilisation of any country by its power of production. The end is considered to be attained when we arrive at counting by millions the tons of iron which have been wrought, the yards of manufactured cottons, or the tale of exports and imports. In such a country, the wealthy lay the whole world under contribution for the adornment of their palaces, and the laying of their tables. In their cities, by the blazing gas-lights, behind sheets of plate-glass, are spread the glittering cut brilliants, finely-wrought gold, or silks of a thousand colours. And yet a million of paupers are supported by official relief; a third of the population is entirely illiterate, another third is without the necessaries of life, and there is a talk of enlarging the prisons and proclaiming martial law. It is no matter; *this is the most civilised country in the world.* In another country you may see honest country folks, owning their houses and fields, winning by their own labour all that is necessary for themselves. No one is without a certain degree of ease and education. But nowhere is there any luxury. *This is considered a very back-ward country.* Such are the judgments passed habitually nowadays. To my thinking they are false and superficial, and produce the most fatal consequences.

Man has a twofold existence, and therefore two kinds of needs; needs of the body, or corporeal needs; needs of the mind, or intellectual needs. He who lives for his senses only will not hesitate, if he can command by his riches or his power the work of thousands of men, to employ it in satisfying all his fancies, driven, it may be, to the pitch of insanity by the insatiable pursuit of enjoyment, "lassata sed non satiata." He, on the contrary, who cultivates the life of the mind, will have few material wants, and may even come to neglecting the most primary ones. Take on the one hand Heliogabolus, or, better still, that arch-type of imperial Rome in her sensuality and luxury, Trimalcion. On the other, see John the Baptist, living on locusts and wild honey; or Saint Paul, earning his bread by tent-making, as Spinoza did later on by polishing the glass of watches.

The greatest of artists, Michael Angelo, once said to his friend Condivi: "I, though I am rich, have always lived like a poor man." "Yes," said Condivi to him, "you have always lived like a poor man, because you have always given away like a rich man." In which of these types do we find the highest moral development?

A certain level of culture creates wants, a still higher level retrenches them. All that administers to rational needs is legitimate and good, because we must maintain the efficiency of our bodily forces, since without them intellectual work becomes difficult or impossible. But all that is yielded to spurious needs is immoral and bad, because it is so much time taken of one's own and of others, which might be better employed. The great Reformers who have changed the whole direction of thought in any country—Moses, Socrates, Buddha, Jesus—have all lived on very little. It is not at the shrine of luxury that the flame is kindled which will purify humanity. We may almost go so far as to say that moral greatness is, not in proportion, but in inverse ratio to wants.

M. Renan has written a page on this subject which is not easily forgotten. "The mistake lies," he says, "not in proclaiming industry to be good and useful, but in attaching too much importance to the pursuit of perfection in certain details. In minor matters, once a good thing has been produced, it is little worth while to improve upon it indefinitely. For if the aim of human life is happiness, this has been very well realised in the past without these superfluities, and if, as the wise think with good reason, it is moral and intellectual grandeur which alone is necessary, these accessories contribute very little to it. History affords us examples of high intellectual attainments and a golden age of happiness which have been reached by men whose material state was crude enough. The Brahmans in India, while still living, as far as exterior civilisation was concerned, on the level of the most backward societies, attained an order of philosophical speculation which Germany alone in our days has been able to surpass. The ideal of the Gospels, unique and unsurpassable, in which the moral sense is wrought out with the most marvellous delicacy, takes us into the midst of a life as simple as that of our rural solitudes, a life in which the complications of exterior things find but little place. Far from the progress of art running parallel with the progress made by any nation in the taste for the comforts of life, we may say, without paradox, that those times and those countries in which the comforts of life have become the main object of society, have been the least highly gifted in the things of art." ("Essays on Morals and Criticism.")

CHAPTER VI.

IS LUXURY NECESSARY FOR THE SAKE OF KEEPING MACHINERY EMPLOYED?

WE will now turn to another set of considerations. Bastiat, who in many of his writings preaches moderation of desires, is yet driven, as it were in spite of himself, in his "Economic Harmonies," to justify luxury, and that for a reason which seems to be a very serious one. "It is not possible," he says, " to find a satisfactory solution to the problems of machinery, of foreign competition, and of luxury, so long as we regard wants as an invariable quantity, and pay no heed to their indefinite capacity for expansion." To solve economic problems then, according to Bastiat, we must urge men

48

incessantly to multiply and refine their wants, thus setting political economy entirely at variance with the whole of moral teaching, both ancient and modern. Bastiat sees this. "I hear you say," he proceeds, "Economist, you are caught tripping already. You announced that your science was in agreement with morality, and here you are justifying sybaritism,"—which in fact he does.

What is his reply to this objection? "And you, austere philosopher and preacher of morals, are you content with satisfying the needs of primitive man?" But this is no answer at all. No matter what the philosopher may do, Bastiat himself, there is no doubt, as he himself puts it, declares sybaritism to be necessary.

Let us see how he is led into this deplorable contradiction, which does, it must be confessed, appear to result from the doctrines of the orthodox Political Economy. Machinery economises labour; the more,

D

therefore, machines are increased and perfected, the fewer hours of labour are needed to obtain the same products. To diminish the hours of work means to diminish the demand for hands, and to throw out of employment an increasing number of workers. In order that they may be kept supplied with occupation, it is necessary that, in proportion as actual wants are satisfied with less effort, new wants should arise to utilize those hours of labour which the perfecting of mechanical engines and technical processes has left to be disposed of anew. It thus appears that the indefinite expansiveness of wants is indispensable, for without it the indefinite progress of science and mechanics must suppress an ever-increasing number of workers. This is, in point of fact, the spectacle presented to us by economic development. In proportion as the necessaries of life were more easily obtainable, spurious needs arose for this countless array of elegant and costly trifles which encumber our shops, and are bought by an ever larger circle of consumers. Short of suppressing machinery, there is thus no course left to us but either to press on to sybaritism, or else to resign ourselves to the extinction of a constantly increasing number of workers. It is thus that a certain school of Political Economy sets itself at variance with traditional morality.

As I cannot admit that the moralists of antiquity and the fathers of the Church were wrong in urging us to limit our appetites and our desires, I believe that there must be a solution to the problem of machinery other than that indicated by Bastiat. And this, I believe, is the following:—

Machinery, producing more quickly, can ensure to us *either* more products or more leisure. I maintain that, when our rational wants are satisfied, what we need is not to create a superfluity for the satisfaction of spurious needs, but to apply our leisure to the cultivation of our minds, and to the enjoyment of the society of our fellows, and of the beauties of nature and art. I compare humanity to Robinson Crusoe on his island. At first, he must work from morning till night, merely to keep himself alive; later on, by means of all kinds of improved machinery, he can produce, in six hours of work a day, everything that his rational wants demand. Will he proceed to use the six additional hours, now placed at his disposal, in wearying himself further for the sake of clothing himself in ribbons and velvets, in brocaded silks and laces? No, the higher he stands in elevation of mind and in culture, the less he will think of such childishness. He will desire only to enjoy God, nature, and himself.

Machinery has been called the liberator of humanity. This is not so if machinery is to plunge us deeper in the mire of matter by carrying sensuality to a finer pitch; but it will be true if it sets humanity free from a great part of that severe labour, at the price of which it gains its existence. "It is doubtful," says John Stuart Mill, "whether all our machinery has diminished by one hour the labour of a single human being." Not only so, but men toil nowadays more than ever before. Of old, night brought men "sweet sleep and the oblivion of cares," as says the Latin poet. Nowadays, in consequence of the greater activity of industry, how many are there who work all night long in mines, in sugar factories, on steamers, on railways, in postal and telegraph services; and, indeed, I know not where besides? As Hamlet says: "What might be toward that this sweaty haste doth make the night joint labourer with the day?" Life in our civilised countries has grown far more intense, and the expenditure of nervous force far greater. We all, from the summit of the social ladder to its base, from the cabinet minister, who succumbs under the mass of business which overwhelms him, to the miner at the bottom of the coal-pit, are becoming the slaves of a gigantic social engine whose motion constantly accelerates. It is not thus that machinery will enfranchise the human race. It *ought* to secure men, first, the more and more easy satisfaction of their rational wants; and next, more leisure, with, as a consequence, a higher intellectual culture.

But, you will say, what are these "rational wants" of which you speak so often? Who is to mark the limit? Do you wish us once more to live on acorns, and clothe ourselves with the skins of animals?

By rational wants I understand those that reason supports, and hygiene determines. The latter can tell us with great exactness what nourishment, what clothing, and what kind of lodging is most suited to each season and to any given climate. To this add those inexpensive accessories that the progress of ndustry already places within reach of every one's purse. J. B. Say defines luxury, rightly, as I think, as " the use of those things that are rare and costly. A thing that is costly represents much labour ano much time. If it only satisfies a spurious want, we are wrong in ordering it. There is no difficulty in fixing the limit between rational and irrational methods of consumption. Is the satisfaction which this article affords you worth the time and effort necessary for its production? This is the question which must be asked in deciding each particular case.

M. Baudrillart holds that luxury consists mainly in what is superfluous. I agree rather with J. B. Say that it consists in what is very costly. To take some examples given by M. Baudrillart; a penny Japanese fan, or a mirror costing a few shillings, are, perhaps, superfluities; but since they cost but a very small amount of labour, the satisfaction they give is worth this little sacrifice. When the cultivator drinks his own wine which he could sell, perhaps, at eightpence a gallon, this is not luxury. When a millionaire drinks Johannisberg wine at 32s. a bottle, the expense for him relatively is less ; but he consumes the equivalent of twenty days' work. These twenty days, taken from the whole time which humanity has to satisfy its primary needs, of what avail were they ? They availed only to secure the fugitive enjoyment of a certain flavour which it is difficult even for the most delicate palates to appreciate. No one can hesitate to pronounce this time wasted. But the fact escapes general recognition under the complex phenomena of exchange, though, already, it is beginning to be understood : already the generality of men cry shame at certain forms of foolish spending, even when committed by those who can afford it without ruining themselves. "It is a waste which cries out for vengeance," we hear it said. It is, indeed, a waste of men's time, seeing that so many suffer too often from cold and hunger.

When the eye of God beholds our earth, and on it millions of men engaged in manufacturing useless things, such as jewels and laces, or harmful things like opium and spirits, side by side with millions of other men in the extremity of want, how foolish, how infantile, how barbarous must we appear to Him! We pass our time in making ribbons and trinkets, and we have not sufficient food or clothing! The fathers of the Church came to this same conclusion, guided by the light of the Gospels, and so did the fathers of Political Economy, taught by the inductions of science, before the sophistries by which luxury is justified had poisoned the pulpits of our Church and the chairs of our Universities.

CHAPTER VII.

THREE ASPECTS OF THE QUESTION OF LUXURY.

LUXURY may be considered from three different points of view. First, as a question of morals, for the individual as such: Within what limits is the effort to satisfy wants favourable to the normal development of human faculties? Secondly, as a question of economics: To what extent does luxury serve to advance or hinder the accumulation of wealth? Thirdly, as a question of right and justice: Is luxury compatible with the equitable distribution of products, and with the principle that each man's remuneration should be in proportion to the amount of useful labour accomplished by him?

The third aspect of the problem has scarcely ever yet been touched upon. It has hitherto not been clearly recognised that the principles of justice ought to be applied to economic distribution. It must not be forgotten, however, that Christian teaching, which makes charity a positive duty, has always condemned luxury, seeing that it leads men to squander in useless, and therefore unjustifiable, superfluities what ought rather to be given to the poor.

CHAPTER VIII.

LUXURY AND THE IDEAL LIFE.

WE will first deal with luxury from the point of view of the individual. Is it beneficial to him or the reverse? Let us put aside for the present all considerations which concern his fellows, and the duties towards them which justice and charity demand. To answer the above question, we must determine wherein consists human well-being, and what is the aim and destiny of man. Clearly the end to be attained is the normal development of all his faculties, and the happiness which ensues therefrom.

Here the pessimists will arrest me, perhaps, by

saying that the more our faculties are developed, the more they become sources of suffering to us; that "the man who thinks is a depraved animal;" that the brute is happier than the so-called lord of creation; that the plant is still happier than the brute, and the mineral than the plant; and in fine, that Nonentity, or the Buddhist Nirvana, is the supreme felicity.

But I shall not pause to discuss here the doctrines of Pessimism. Whatever Schopenhauer and Hartmann may say, it seems difficult to believe that all this immense evolution starting from matter, diffiuse and amorphic, to result, after an infinite series of transformations, in conscious personality and human intelligence—it is difficult, I say, to believe that this vast process is nothing but an uninterrupted progress in misery, leading up to final despair. From the first beginnings of life, every being aspires to self-preservation and perpetuation, to constant growth and expansion. It is the universal law of life, and the conviction seems forced upon us that its accomplishment *must* be attended with satisfaction and achieved with gladness. We must therefore strive towards perfection; and even were it true that our happiness does not increase in proportion as we approach nearer to it, might we not see in this the proof that our destiny is not to be accomplished entirely in this life on earth?

Perfection for man consists in the full development of all his forces, physical and intellectual, and of all his emotions, his family affection and love of humanity, his sense of the beautiful in nature and in art.

Here we find ourselves confronted with two different types of human perfection: the Christian type, and the type conceived by the ancients. The ideal of Christian perfection appears to me to be the higher in all that concerns our duties to our fellows,

our brothers, as it holds them, and in all those prac-
tices it imposes, of justice and of charity, which
the ancient philosophers saw only in confused and
uncertain outlines. But the Christian ideal neglects
the physical man. This is because it grew up
imbued with the idea that the world was shortly to
come to an end, and it, therefore, had only in view
"the kingdom of heaven which is at hand." This
it was which gave to the whole Christian conception
of life the ascetic colouring which has been so often
objected against it. It arose naturally enough as
a consequence of these ideas concerning the end of
the world. If this world is to come to an end
speedily, as the early Christians believed, and if
"the Lord will come in His kingdom before this
generation pass away," as the Gospel, or Good News
of the approaching new creation, foretold, no prudent
man can do other than make preparation for this
coming event. It is not therefore to the rule of

ascetic Christianity that we must look for guidance as to the true life of the individual. If we took it literally it would reduce us to the life of the Anchorite, or even of a Stylite.

It is to Greece that we must look for an example here. The young Greek cultivates by constant exercise both the muscles of his body and the faculties of his mind. He passes his mornings in the Gymnasium, his afternoons in the open air, conversing with philosophers and sages. He thus achieves the desired ideal, "mens sana in corpore sano." As Herbert Spencer justly says in his excellent book on "Education," the essential thing is to "maintain sound health, for of what avail are rank, honours, and wealth, to an invalid or a valetudinarian?" Greek life then must be our model, as it has been in the English universities. The only thing it lacks is manual labour, which among the Greeks devolved upon slaves. This was a grave mistake, nay, let us rather say a grave crime, for it was the violation of a natural law, and as such was punished by inevitable decay. Nature demands work from all. We all have certain needs, and we are all supplied with organs, and an intelligence to direct them in procuring the satisfaction of these needs. All organic beings live thus by personal effort. If we shift off upon others all the labour necessary to procure our subsistence, we are inevitably punished by anæmia, by dyspepsia, by melancholy, by spleen; in a word, by all the evils which spring from idleness and ennui. The man who desires to preserve as long as possible his health and strength by obedience to the laws of nature will exact from himself and regularly perform some kind of bodily exercise. The ancients were careful to do this: a good part of each day they devoted to strengthening and exercising their muscles in the bath or on the field of Mars. For the modern

E

man who has no slaves to serve him, gymnastic exercises of no particular economic value ought to be supplemented by the practice of arms, and by some really useful kind of manual labour. This at once preserves him from effeminacy and ultra-refinement.

Life among the ancients was elegant, but simple. At Athens and at Rome, even the man of ease and wealth did not crowd his house with such a quantity of objects as is considered indispensable by us to-day. Enter one of the houses at Pompeii; you can there understand at a glance the way the ancients understood life, and the manner in which they lived it. First and foremost, they sought the beautiful in everything, and in everything gave it the first place. Art beautified everything, forums, baths, temples, every part of a private house, court, garden, walls, furniture, and even the humblest kitchen utensils. But they had few needs, and but little means of satisfying them. Their bedrooms were like convent-cells, with only room for a bed, a chair, and a small chest, which would not even contain the wardrobe of a working-man of to-day. Their garments were as simple as those of the religious orders, consisting of a linen tunic and a simple woollen cloak, which was nothing but a plain piece of stuff draped on the shoulders. Hence, it is easy to see why they had no wardrobes. Changes of fashion were unknown, and their costume remained the same for more than a thousand years. In their repasts, too, the ancients were simple and abstemious. Think of how Horace was wont to sup, Horace who was yet an epicurean—

" Vivitur parvo bene cui paternum
Splendet in mensa tenui Salinum."

Carm. ii. 16.

"That man lives happily at a small cost who sees on his frugal table the shining salt-box of his fathers."

In another passage, speaking of his meals, he says :

" Inde domum me
Ad porri et ciceris refero laganique catinum."

Sat. i. 6, 115.

"Then I go home to my dish of leeks or peas, or it may be some fritters."

Or again—

" O quando faba Pythagoræ cognata simulque
Uncta satis pingui ponentur oluscula lardo ?"

Sat. ii. 6, 63.

"O when will the bean, first cousin to Pythagoras, appear on my table, and fine herbs seasoned with rich bacon-fat ?"

At Athens, people of the highest rank lived on very little, as the Neapolitans do to-day. Each could say with the philosopher, "Omnia mecum porto." "I carry my all on my person." Those giant repasts of Trimalcion, and the extravagant expenditure of some of the emperors, are the fruit of the madness of absolute power. We find nothing of the kind in Greece, or even at Rome in ordinary life. In those days a man's wants being few in number, he could devote all his time to the cultivation of his faculties, to æsthetic pleasures or cares of State, to gymnastics or philosophy, to literature or politics, or the drama.

Modern luxury and the thousand and one requirements of modern comfort are attended by a twofold
inconvenience. First, there is valuable time wasted
in making the money which is spent on these useless
trifles, and then there is the waste of the little leisure
that remains on spending it. The whole man is thus
drawn into the vortex of material pursuits; nothing
is left of him for the life of the mind and heart.
Look at the existence of a financier who counts
his millions by tens. His affairs generally, his
calculations, his clients, his colleagues take up his
whole day; and in the evening also, in the midst of
all those pleasures for the sake of which he pursues
this chase for wealth, he is still dreaming of new
operations by which he may increase a fortune whose
revenues already are sufficient to cover a thousand
times over all the wants that he can imagine or conceive. He is like one overwhelmed by the weight of
his possessions. No doubt, he is useful as a wheel in

the vast machinery of production; but is he walking in the path that leads to happiness and to perfection?

"At Paris, you may see a man who has enough to live upon till the day of judgment, but who yet works incessantly and runs the risk of shortening his days for the sake of increasing his means." ("Montesquieu, Lettres Persanes.") This is the kind of life led by those princes of opulence at New York, Astor, Vanderbilt and Stewart, each of whom left a fortune of more than £20,000,000.

The man of few wants has few cares. He is as gay as the sky-lark or Lafontaine's cobbler who sings from early dawn. Thanks to the marvels of science and mechanics, we produce in these days so much wealth that the figures which measure it for the statistician are so large as to amaze us—and yet ours is an age of sadness, of pre-occupation and overstrain. Men do not laugh as once they laughed, nor find amusement where once they found it. There is effort and anxiety everywhere, and everywhere men over-reach and deceive each other.

Bossuet speaks on this point in his "Treatise on Concupiscence," and one cannot fail to admire the force and grandeur of his language. "The body it is," he says, "which drags us down from the loftier levels of thought, which chains us to the earth, when we ought to be breathing the pure air of heaven." Listen again to the great preacher, as he shows us in a word what should be the goal of all our efforts: "Why will you turn your very necessities into vanity? You must have a house to protect you from the air which might injure you; but this is your weakness. You need nourishment to repair your forces, which waste and consume every moment; another weakness. You need a bed to lie on when you are tired, where you may seek the slumber which swathes and enfolds your reason: another deplorable weakness. And all these needs, which are but witnesses and proofs of your miserable weakness, you turn into means of displaying your vanity, as if you would exult in the very infirmities which compass you on every side."

We sometimes find Bossuet pushing the doctrine of self-denial to the extent of asceticism, but at bottom must we not admit that he is right? Is not every one of our needs a weakness, a subservience to infirmity, and a temptation to sacrifice true well-being and the pursuit of right to sensuality? Dignity of life, uprightness of conduct, fidelity to principle—are not these most often to be found in conjunction with great simplicity of living? The fewer one's wants, the more one is free to follow the dictates of duty, and the less one is likely to be influenced by the promptings of cupidity in important matters, such as the choice of a career, of a wife, or of a political party.

In England, we are told by Helvetius in his book,

"On Mind," a cabinet minister went one day to a member of the opposition in the House of Commons in order to buy his vote, as was then the custom frequently practised. He found the member dining on a shoulder of mutton, and drinking only water, and the response he met with was, "I should have thought the simplicity of my repast might have saved me the insult of your offer."

The memory of the greatest orator of the French Revolution is tarnished by his venality. Why did Mirabeau consent to touch a pension out of the king's privy purse, if it was not to keep up his luxury and his dissolute life? Whatever may be said against him, I admire Jean Jacques Rousseau for obstinately refusing all the gifts that were offered him, and continuing to live in his little room on the proceeds of his music copying.

Diogenes one day saw a man drinking water from the palm of his hand, and immediately threw away his bowl to do likewise. Economically, he was wrong, for there is more satisfaction and less trouble in drinking from a glass than from one's hand; but the idea upon which he acted was, in my opinion, sensible enough.

When discussing this question of luxury one day I expressed a wish that instead of having feet which we must constantly protect from stones and thorns as well as from damp, we might have horses' hoofs, and so dispense with shoes and stockings and all their attendant discomforts. I was laughed at for this idea, and it was nicknamed "Sabotism" (sabot=hoof). But I persist in believing with Bossuet that our needs are so many weaknesses which divert us from the ideal and overwhelm us in worldly interests. Without wants, we might be like the lilies of the Gospel, "which toil not, neither do they spin," or we might even resemble those persons of independent means who pass from one delightful spot to another, enjoying at their ease the beauties of nature.

I am not forgetting that man is so constituted that in his present existence work is for him a necessary condition of physical and moral health ; but is it not desirable, to say the least, that this work should be distributed in such a manner as to be nowhere so prolonged or so arduous as to brutalize him ?

Self-denial should not be allowed to go to the length of producing coarseness of manners or a numbed state of intelligence, still less, to the apotheosis of dirt, as in the case of St. Labre ; or to self-mutilations, as practised by the fakirs : but of these things we need have no fear, our age has no leanings in this direction. The universal bent is towards a refinement of sensuality, and it is this growing tendency that we need to combat.

Let us have the courage to set up as models, Socrates, whose vigorous frame, when in the army, endured heat, cold and fatigue better than the veterans, and who being without wants lived only for philosophy and justice; or, again, St. Paul, enduring without shrinking every kind of trial—imprisonment, stripes, shipwreck, poverty, "many deaths"—for the service of truth. The soul of an apostle in a frame of iron—this is what we must hold up to the admiration of our age, and the imitation of our rising generation; not the pursuit of an over-refined luxury for the pampering of enervated tastes, and senses blunted by satiety.

CHAPTER IX.

LUXURY IN RELATION TO THE PROSPERITY OF NATIONS.

WE have in the next place to consider luxury from the point of view of national prosperity, and to ask ourselves if it has a favourable influence on it, as some maintain.

It is on this point that the most dangerous form of error is current. Those who indulge in large expenditure on luxuries flatter themselves that they are thereby benefiting their fellows, especially of the labouring class; and the governing classes seem to have the same idea, for there are certain functionaries who are allowed special grants for the express purpose of setting an example of this kind of dissipation. The most elementary notions of Political Economy show how completely fallacious is this idea.

The progress of industry depends on the growth of capital, and capital comes by saving. The waste of money which luxury entails is the very reverse of saving, and so far from giving an impulse to industry, it retards it. We must here recall the wise remark of John Stuart Mill: the demand for any commodity does not furnish the means of producing it. I may wish this year to buy some velvet, to manufacture which machines are required, and all kinds of mechanical appliances. My demand will not furnish this necessary capital. This must be contributed by some-one who, instead of consuming, has been saving. We can therefore be useful to the working-classes, and we can give them work to do, not by ourselves consuming, but by increasing their consumption, while they produce the tools, engines, and preliminary appliances necessary for a new manufacture.

So far from contributing to raise wages, luxury retards their rise. When is it that the wages of the working-classes rise, in point of fact? It is when capital increases more rapidly than the number of workmen, or, as Cobden puts it, when two masters run after one man. But for two masters to compete over one man in the labour market, both must first have accumulated capital by saving. It is therefore by saving, and not by expensive luxury, that it becomes possible to start new manufactures, and thus to employ more workmen.

No doubt, in very rich countries luxury does not, as a matter of fact, prevent the growth of capital, since the national revenues are large enough to suffice for both. Side by side with

the spendthrifts, we find the men who save
and who accumulate. When a man has a yearly
income which he counts by millions, he can indulge a good many fancies and still make considerable savings every year. Before the recent
financial crisis the annual increase of capital in
England was estimated at about 120 millions
sterling. This increase was employed in the creation
of new enterprises, not in England only, but all
over the world. Moreover, can there be any doubt
but that, if the practice of saving were yet more
general, the rise in value of the whole amount of
productive capital and the general growth of industry would attain still higher proportions?

"But," it will be said, "at least you will not
deny that luxury is good for trade. This is an
axiom which every one admits."

J. B. Say tells a story *a propos* of this. When
at college he used to spend his sundays at the

house of an uncle of his who went in for good living seasoned with philanthropy. One day at dessert the said uncle, having emptied an old bottle of choice wine, broke his glasses with the remark: "Everyone must get a living." This incident set young Say thinking. He asked himself why, if his uncle wished to make a livelihood for the workmen, he did not break up all the glass and crockery on his table, as well as his furniture and his window-panes? By this means he would give still more employment. On the same plea it follows that Nero was inspired by true economic principles when he sang over the spectacle of Rome in flames.

An economic writer of the time of the restoration in France, and a professed champion of Protection, by name Saint-Chamant, supposes the case of the destruction of Paris by fire. As a citizen, he deplores the calamity; but as an economist he rejoices over it.

F

He thinks it an excellent thing for labour, to which it cannot fail to give a tremendous impulse.

Now, this is the conclusion to which we are inevitably driven, so long as we regard not the result of labour, but only labour in itself. This is the fallacy which Bastiat has aptly called *Sisyphism.* Political Economy, if it proceeded on these lines, would be the science, not of the production, but of the destruction of wealth. It is evident that there is some mistake here, and it is important that this should be clearly disentangled, and once for all refuted.

To quote Bastiat again : " We must distinguish what we see from what we do not see." What we see is the workman replacing what has been destroyed : what we do not see is *another workman producing other articles which might have been paid for by the money thus employed.* Let us admit, as the English proverb says, that " it is an ill wind that blows nobody any good," or again, "that every dark cloud has a silver lining." No doubt, when J. B. Say's uncle broke his glasses, he gave the glass manufactory work in supplying him with others. But if he had not spent the money thus, he might have bought some chairs and tables, or some new and finer glass, by which means he would have given as much in wages and have had more goods himself. His own wealth, and consequently that of his country, would have been increased.

At Paris the monuments which were burnt in 1871 are being rebuilt; undoubtedly this has given occupation to many trades, but with the millions spent on this the French might have raised other monuments, or established schools, or laid down many leagues of railroad. Ultimately, Paris would have still had her monuments and palaces, while France would have gained in addition new educational premises, or new means of transport, which, as it is, she will only obtain at the price of new sacrifices.

"This is all very well," our opponents insist, "but with these fine theories of yours, which are descended in a direct line from the Porticoes, from the Thebaïd, or even from the tub of Diogenes, you would bring starvation on thousands of tradesmen and of artisans."

Let us examine this objection by the light of an example. A rich banker devotes £40,000 a year to dinners, balls, and entertainments of every kind, and he induces those whom he invites to spend perhaps three times as much again. The purveyors of fashions, the tailors, milliners, hair-dressers, and provision dealers, do a thriving trade and make their golden pile. The public is delighted. "Trade is brisk." There comes on the scene a preacher imbued, not with the lax theories of the Church of to-day, but with the holy rigour of the early fathers. He thunders against luxury. Society listens, is touched; society reforms. No more balls, no more festivities. Austerity is the prevailing *régime;* society seems made up of quakers. What will be the result of so great a change?

It is clear that the banker and all his tribe are not going to throw all their money into the river. What will they do with it? One thing is certain, they will want to make a profit on it. How, then? One has an outlying property long neglected; this he improves, plants, and drains; he repairs the buildings on it, and makes roads. Another has a factory which he will enlarge. A third takes rail-way shares, and thus, indirectly, lays down some yards of railroad. In a word, every one of them will set labour in motion, and labour of a useful and productive kind, since they count on securing interest on their investments. The same amount of money will be spent—for nowadays it is not the fashion to bury one's gold underground. The same amount of labour is set in motion, the same number of workmen fed; but these are at work in the country where we do not see them, and no longer in the hair-dresser's shop, or behind the counter, or in the show-room, where they were constantly in view. There is therefore no suppression of labour, but it is diverted into new channels.

But let us consider what difference this will make to the wealth of the country. When the lights of the ball-room are put out, and the entertainer has seen the last of his guests, what remains to show for it? Nothing, unless it be the stings of wounded vanity, the discomforts of an uneasy digestion, the restlessness of over-strained nerves. Social capital has diminished in two senses—in commodities, and in human strength. But in the other case supposed, when the useful works, which gave as much employment, are terminated, there remains a field, well drained and manured, which will yield more corn; a forest, better planted, which will give more wood; a new machine set up which will turn out more manufactured articles; a new line of railway constructed which will carry men and merchandise at cheaper rates. The country will be enriched and will produce the more. Consequently, in the following year the workman will be better off. The price of commodities will diminish, and to work the increased capital there will be a demand for fresh hands; wages will rise. There will thus be profit on both sides.

But there are yet other advantages. I have hitherto supposed the same amount of capital, divested from expenditure on luxury into useful channels, to be able to maintain only the same number of labourers in the country as it had done in town. But it will, in point of fact, support a larger number, for wages being lower and living less ex-

pensive in the country, the same money will pay
more workmen. In the second place, the production
of useful commodities and of the necessaries of life is
much more stable than that of luxuries, which can
be more readily dispensed with upon occasion.
When public confidence is shaken, at the time of any
political or economic crisis, and the revenue is de-
clining, it will be in the direction of these factitious
wants that economies will first be practised, by which
means the workmen engaged in the manufacture of
luxuries will be thrown out of employment. Also
the changes of fashion will no longer be productive
of such suffering as at present. I have often seen in
Flanders young girls and children making what is
known as Valenciennes lace. The fashion changes in
favour of Brussels lace, Alençon or Venetian point;
and these busy workers have their wages lowered
to a point which brings hunger and suffering upon
them. Nothing is more heart-breaking than to see

the spindle in these delicate, skilful, and most industrious fingers paralysed by the caprice of some celebrated dressmaker. Thus luxury not only arrests the accumulation of capital, but also employs less labour, and that of a more precarious and irregular kind, than the production of useful commodities.

"But all the same," I hear some one say, "money must circulate." Nonsense again, I answer. The circulation in itself is not what matters. Money circulates nowhere more rapidly than at the gaming table. Millions are there lost and won, but wherein is the country the richer? Money will always circulate, at least, as long as you do not bury it in an old pot; the important point is whether in passing from hand to hand it has realised an equivalent in permanent improvements and the satisfaction of real human wants, or whether, instead of this, it has created the mass of useless trifles in which the sensual, the vain, and the frivolous take delight.

On some great occasion we give a display of fireworks which cost £8,000. The philosopher, the theologian, and the economist disapprove; the idlers look on and applaud. "Does not the money remain in the country?" This is folly and nothing else. No doubt the money remains, but wealth to the amount that it represents has been dissipated. There were here two kinds of capital, the one in money, the other in powder. This powder might have been used for the extraction of coal or other minerals from the earth, or for tunnelling a hill or an isthmus for the passage of trains or vessels. When the fireworks have gone off, nothing remains but the money. The second capital has vanished in smoke. To consume is always to destroy. What we have to insist on is that this destruction should give, as compensation, satisfaction to real wants, or the creation of some new means of production.

All consumption is, at bottom, a form of exchange.

You give a certain actual value: what do you get in exchange? Bodily strength and mental nourishment? then you have struck a good bargain. The means of exciting pride and vanity, which are less than nothing worth? then you have bargained badly.

It follows from what has been said above that the State pursues a senseless and blameworthy policy in encouraging its functionaries by grants "for cost of representation" to set an example of luxury; for by this means it puts a check on the growth of capital; hence on industry and on the rise of wages. It is desirable, on the contrary, for those who represent public authority to lead simple and even austere lives. With a view to this, the democracies of Switzerland and the United States of America make less difference in the amount of salaries. The lower grades are more highly paid, and the superior less than with us.

Economists have unsparingly denounced, and with

good reason, the subsidies paid to theatres by large towns on the Continent. I would allow the most ample expenditure for the spread of light and knowledge of healthy notions of morality, or the taste for the beautiful. But who would dare to say that the stage as it now is, except at such places as the Theatre Français, has any share in forming taste and elevating the mind ? As Rousseau says, in his letter to d'Alembert on theatres, "public money is spent in opening schools of bad examples and a hot-bed of corrupt manners." Is it just that the poor should pay for the pleasure of the rich, and that contributions should be levied on all to assure ticket-holders their seats at half-price ? Too often what is really wanted, instead of a public grant, is a suppression of the license on the score of injury to public morality. Here again it is generally pleaded that theatrical displays "circulate money and are good for trade." We have already exposed the pernicious fallacies contained in this plea.

Owing to the fact that economic analysis had not in those days displayed the absurdity of these notions, we find many contradictory statements on this subject in writers of the 18th century. Voltaire in several passages condemns luxury; but in the "Mondain" and others of his writings he extols it, owing to the influence exerted on him by the then celebrated "Fable of the Bees," which is an elaborate apology for luxury. In Montesquieu this incoherence and hesitancy is still more marked. He goes to the root of the matter, and sees clearly that luxury is a cause of demoralisation and decay, and yet he is paralysed in his denunciation of it by the belief, which he shared with all his century, that luxury is a source of wealth. Thus he says: "Fashion is an important matter; the increasing frivolity of men's minds is ever multiplying new branches of trade." Voltaire reproduces the same idea in his defence of the worldling :—

> " Sachez surtout que le luxe enrichit
>   Un grand Etat, s'il en perd un petit.
>   Le pauvre y vit de vanités des grands."

" Know then that luxury, my friends, which ruins the small State,
Will bring prosperity and wealth and splendour to the great ;
The rich man's vanities become the poor man's livelihood."

La Fontaine, too, echoes the universal misconception :

> " Je ne sais d'homme nécessaire
>   Que celui dont le luxe épand beaucoup de biens.
>   Nous en usons, Dieu soit.   Nôtre plaisir occupe
>   L' artisan, le vendeur . . . ."

" I know no man so necessary as he whose luxury scatters treasures everywhere.   Heaven only knows how much we consume !   But our pleasures give occupation to the artisan and tradesman."

Even Rousseau thinks that "luxury may be necessary to give the poor a livelihood."   But he, it is true, goes on to say: "Yet if there were no luxury, there would be no poor."

It is of paramount importance to uproot from the public mind this fundamental error of believing that luxury is economically useful, because it feeds labour. Let it be clearly understood that ostentation, idleness, and debauchery fritter away the resources which might otherwise be so advantageously utilized. The precepts of morality will not, it is to be feared, meet with an immediate response; but, at least, let no one flatter himself in future that in cutting the corn before it is ripe, and devouring capital at its source, he is rendering a service to his fellow-men.

Sismondi in his "New Principles of Political Economy" (Bk. ii. Ch. 2.) makes this statement:—"If the wealthy classes suddenly resolved to live by labour as the poor do, and to add their income to their capital, the working-classes would be brought to desperation, and would die of starvation very soon." Sismondi forgets that in order to add their income to their capital they would have to spend it on machines, or on agricultural improvements, in investments of every kind, and that thus they would give employment to as many workmen as in buying useless luxuries.

It is, however, true that any sudden change in the direction of the revenue would ruin those to whom it had previously given a livelihood, supposing them to be unable to perform the new kinds of labour required. It would therefore be desirable that the change should be accomplished gradually. But there is no reason to fear as yet that the wealthy classes will all at once betake themselves to russet gowns and coarse broth.

CHAPTER X.

LUXURY AND JUSTICE.

WE have said that there was a third aspect in which we must regard luxury : namely, in its rela- tion to law and equity. We must in fact ask ourselves whether luxury is compatible with justice ? The whole of Christian tradition, from its source downwards, answers this question in the negative. How many passages might we not cite from the Gospels to this effect! Lazarus is received into Abraham's bosom, while the rich man is cast into torments. "It is easier for a camel—or a cable of camel's hair—to pass through the needle's eye, than for a rich man to enter into the Kingdom of God."

" Woe unto them that are rich, for they find their happiness in this world." Luxury, which is the selfish and unprincipled use of wealth, thus stands absolutely condemned by Christian ethics.

The fathers of the Church recognise a kind of equality of rights. Those who have a superfluity of wealth cannot lawfully spend it all on themselves. It is their duty to share it with those who lack even the bare necessaries of life. As Salvien says, " the rich is only the steward of the poor." M. Baudrillart quotes a passage from a sermon of Bourdaloue on Almsgiving in which this doctrine is most explicitly set forth: " According to the law of nature," he says, " all things ought to be the common property of all. As all men are equally men, no one man by himself and by his own nature has any rights more extensive or better established than any other. Thus it seemed natural that God should give them the good things of the earth that they might gather its fruits, each according to his present need. . . . When the rich man gives alms, let him not flatter himself on the score of liberality, for in giving it he is but acquitting himself of a debt which the poor can lawfully claim from him, and which he cannot without injustice refuse." The Church, however, has but one remedy to offer for this inequality of conditions and the luxury which results from it: and this remedy is almsgiving, always almsgiving, and nothing else. But what is to be done when Political Economy, by an appeal to facts, demonstrates that almsgiving engenders idleness, mendicity, inertia, and debasement of character, and that when ultimately analysed it is seen to be iniquitous, since it is itself exploited in one form or other, by rent or by taxation, from those who toil for the benefit of those who do not? J. B. Say, who may be called the Adam Smith of France, shows very clearly that a too unequal distribution of wealth is the source of luxury. "The too great inequality of fortunes is hostile to every form of consumption properly so called. It developes imaginary wants, and at the same time real wants are less and less efficiently supplied. The extremity of misery and the surfeit of wealth stand everywhere side by side. The toil wrung from one portion of humanity provides for the needs of the other portion. Splendid colonnades, and loathsome hovels; the rags of poverty, and the exacting demands of luxury; in a word, the most useless profusion in the midst of the most urgent need."

Montesquieu admits with Bourdaloue that "private fortunes have increased only at the cost of a loss of necessary physique to a large part of the nation: this loss, then, must be made good to them." And how does he propose to do this? By certain kinds of expenditure on the part of the rich, to be imposed, if need be, by the Government

The great political writer's solution is even worse than the great pulpit orator's. The authors of the French Revolution, and the compilers of the French Civil Code caught a glimpse of the true solution and endeavoured, though with insufficient logic, perhaps, to follow it up. This solution consists in bringing about such a distribution of wealth as to endow the largest possible number of citizens with property in some shape or form. Let every one hold some property in land or in stocks or debentures; in a word, *a little capital. Democratise property.* The result will be that every man will enjoy the produce of his own labour to the full, and this baneful luxury, which is the inevitable result of extreme inequality, and which is condemned no less by economic science than by Christianity, will altogether disappear. Then, if the progress of mechanics allows of the multiplication and refinement of products, at least they will be brought within the reach of all. This is the state of things which already exists in those countries where civil laws, and the usurpations of feudalism and royalty, have not destroyed the agrarian system or the forms of property handed down from primitive times.

Voltaire, who, like the rest of his contemporaries, said many foolish things on the subject of luxury, has yet a very sensible passage relating to it in his 'Dictionnaire Philosophique." "If by luxury we mean everything over and above what is actually necessary, then luxury is a natural result of human progress; and, to be logical, every one who opposes it ought to believe with Rousseau that the ideal state of happiness and virtue for man is that not even of the savage, but of the ourang-outang. It is felt, however, that it would be absurd to regard as an evil commodities which all men enjoy. The word luxury, therefore, is generally restricted to those superfluities which only a small number of individuals can in-

dulge. In this sense, luxury is a necessary outcome of property—without which no society could
exist—and of a great inequality of fortunes which
is the result, not of proprietary rights in themselves,
but of bad laws. Luxury then is the offspring
of bad laws, and by good laws it may be destroyed.
Moralists should address their sermons to legislators,
and not to private individuals, because it is possible
in this order of things that a man virtuous and enlightened should have power to make reasonable
laws, while it is not to be expected from human
nature that all the rich men of a country should give
up, for virtue's sake, procuring themselves in exchange
for money all the varied enjoyments of the pleasure-
seeking and the vain."

CHAPTER XI.

STATE LUXURY.

THERE is, in my opinion, but one kind of luxury which is justifiable, and that is public or State luxury, and this only on condition that it is well and wisely directed.

M. Baudrillart has some excellent remarks on this subject. Here are some of them:—"From time to time the State will invite the public to enjoy certain pleasures, such as public gardens, fountains, or theatrical displays. Again, it will display the treasures of beauty to multitudes who are cut off from the possession of statuary or paintings. It keeps up museums for the arts, libraries for science and literature, exhibitions and shows for industry. In all its forms, in fact, this collective luxury, if well directed, is profitable to all. It raises the general level and fertilises the genius of production. This kind of luxury furthermore has one striking advantage: it takes away from pomp and display that character of selfishness and isolation which it bears when it is the affair only of private individuals. It places within reach of the many enjoyments which are the habitual portion only of the rich, and which are by them displayed only to a few, and by transient glimpses."

In the last chapter of this book which we have so much quoted, M. Baudrillart examines the question of the reforms to be introduced into State luxury, and his views on this point are very just and very useful. The more democratic society becomes, the more the State is justified in intervening to encourage true art, which is the only form of luxury it should allow itself. At Athens, under Pericles, two

thirds of the revenue was devoted to public monuments. Pindar says in the 7th Olympiad: "In the
day when the Rhodans shall erect an altar to
Minerva, a rain of gold will fall upon the isle." The
golden rain which falls on any people when literature and the fine arts are encouraged as they deserve
to be, is a shower of pure and disinterested delights.

Felix Ravaison justly says, in speaking of *Art in
the Schools* ("Dictionnaire de Pédagogie et d'Instruction Primaire"): "Though education ought at first to
be carried on by means of real things and models,
this is only that these may serve as vehicles to carry
the mind upwards to the sublimest intellectual
heights." Would the baser superfluities, and coarse
and degrading kinds of consumption hold so much
place in the desires of the masses if these could
learn, in ever so small a measure, to take delight in
that kind of divine and healthful intoxication, which
is produced through the ear and through the eye, by

sweet harmonies and by fair proportions? Might not the man of the people, on whom the curse of matter weighs with so heavy a load, find the best kind of alleviation for his hard condition, if his eyes were open to what Leonardo da Vinci calls *la belleza del mondo,* " the beautiful things of the earth;" if he too were thus prepared to enjoy the splendours which he sees profusely scattered through all this vast universe, and which, becoming, as Pascal puts it, perceptible to the heart, will soften his sadness, and give him a presentiment and foretaste of higher destinies?

This is a question which touches on so many different interests that a whole volume might be written upon it. I will not dwell on it further here. I am completely at one with M. Baudrillart in his conclusions on this point, and I believe that statesmen and administrators would find in his book much excellent advice to follow.

CHAPTER XII.

LUXURY AS CONNECTED WITH DIFFERENT FORMS OF GOVERNMENT.

I HAVE still a few words to say on luxury as connected with different forms of government. The subject is so vast that I cannot here do more than touch the fringe of it. M. Baudrillart has a chapter on it, and many of his remarks are profoundly true. But here again I am inclined to be a little more of a puritan than he. He seems to admit that under a monarchy a certain measure of luxury is a necessity. "The monarchy could hardly be supposed to do without external state. A certain amount of this is necessary to monarchical institutions."

Further, he believes that Montesquieu, if he wrote to-day, would no longer say as he does: "In the republics, where there is equality of wealth, there can be no luxury; it is indeed in this very thing that the excellence of a republic consists, and the less luxury there is, the more perfect the republic. In all republics where this equality is not lost sight of, the commercial instinct and the promptings of industry and virtue combined make it possible to every one to live on his own resources, and consequently there is little or no luxury." I believe, on the contrary, that Montesquieu would find, in the general aspect of the world to-day, many good reasons for *not* changing his opinion. There ought not to be luxury either in monarchy or republic.

"We are talking of humanity as it is, and not of humanity as it might be," says M. Baudrillart.

No doubt we must take the actual for our starting-point; but in treating of moral science it is no less certain that our search should be for *what might be,* and above all for *what ought to be.* There.

is an ideal to be pursued; this it is which economists, to my mind, have too often forgotten.

In olden times the pomp and pageant of kings was, no doubt, useful, not to the people, but for the maintenance of the throne; for which, as did the ceremonial of religion, it inspired a superstitious awe and reverence. The sovereign, in the blaze of magnificence which surrounded his throne, appeared as an all-powerful deity. Luxury was one of the bases of power. To-day these splendours no longer have power to impose; they only irritate; this is proved by the response made by the regicides some time ago at Berlin, Madrid, and Naples. "Why did you wish to kill the king?" Passananto was asked. And he replied: "Because he is the chief among the spoilers of the people who are reduced to misery by their exactions. I have no hatred against King Humbert in himself, for he is good and devoted."

Montesquieu thinks that a monarchy must surround itself with luxury and corruption to prevent the people from longing for liberty. The kings of to-day understand that devotion to public ends and simplicity of life are the best titles to the love of their country. King Humbert, like his father, Victor Emmanuel, who was a soldier and huntsman, has a horror of pomp and ceremonial. At Vienna again, while on the "Ring," superb palaces are springing up, the Emperor of Austria continues to live in the old fortress of his ancestors, and he is right in not desiring another. King Leopold of Belgium comes upon his private purse for the means of generously encouraging literature, art, and agriculture, and of furthering that great philanthropic work, the civilisation of Central Africa. Is not Queen Victoria also foolishly reproached for setting an example of economy? The people would be still less likely to forgive luxury in the high dignitaries of a republic than in kings. It would shock them as a kind of scandal, for they would see in it the ostentation of a *parvenu,* whose superfluities would be taken from the necessaries of the workers.

A mischievous notion has become current, to the effect that happiness consists in great wealth. It is for the chiefs of a great republican State to show that the highest functions are compatible with the greatest simplicity, and that they are something quite other than a means of procuring for one's self all the refinements of sensuality and pride.

Montesquieu was right in maintaining that democracy excludes luxury because it discourages extreme inequality. "If in any State," he says, "riches are equally distributed, there will be no luxury, for it is founded only on commodities that one procures through the labour of others."

"History sufficiently shows us," says M. Courcelle-Seneuil, "that luxury springs up only among those who acquire wealth without work—either by gambling, or by war, or by intrigue."

We must not forget that all the ancient democracies perished under the stress of social conflicts. The same danger is always before our eyes, and it breaks out from time to time in fearful catastrophes.

Enlightened by the knowledge of these facts, no writer has understood better than did Aristotle the formidable problem presented by the establishment of a democratic system. In his admirable work, the "Politics," he shows at once the peril and the remedy. "Inequality," he says, "is the source of all revolutions." (Bk. V., chap. i.) "Men being equal in one respect have desired to be in all; equal in liberty, they have desired an absolute equality. Not obtaining it, they are persuaded that they are mulcted of their rights, and raise an insurrection."

The only method, he believes, of preventing insurrections and revolutions is to avoid too great inequality. "Let even the poorest," said he, "have a little inheritance." This is precisely what was effected by the French Revolution, and it is a fact that twice over the established order has been maintained by these very "country folk" with their small inheritances.

It is in this same direction that we must continue to move. The popularisation of property is the only solid basis of democracy. When the head of every family owns a little land, a house, some stocks, or bonds, or some stable source of income, there will no longer be any social revolution to fear. The labouring classes, from their infancy, and in their schools, must be bought to acquire the practice and habit of thrift. The government must facilitate in every possible way the acquisition of property; repeal all the laws which tend to keep it in the hands of a few, and substitute for them laws calculated to bring it within reach of the greatest possible number.

As for the leisured classes, it is their duty to assist this emancipatory movement. A strict application to work, love of the fields and country, simplicity of life, high moral and intellectual culture—these are the examples they must set before the eyes of the people.

Christianity was right: wealth has its obligations. Those who have at their disposal the net produce of the country ought to use their superfluous wealth, not in multiplying and refining material enjoyments, or in exciting the unhealthy promptings of vanity and pride, but in works of public usefulness, as do already many leading citizens in America, and more than one Sovereign in Europe. The Gospel has brought salvation, even in this world. The ancient democracies perished in corruption and civil strife because, being founded on slavery, they could not maintain a just social organisation. Modern democracy will escape these perils if it succeeds in realising the ideal proposed by Christ, and imaged by the Lord's Supper of primitive times—that of true human brotherhood.

Voltaire, on his side, was also right; it will not be the sermons of preachers nor the arguments of economists that will bring about the disappearance of luxury, but the slow and continuous progress of institutions and of laws.

LAW AND MORALS IN POLITICAL
ECONOMY.

CHAPTER I.

POLITICAL ECONOMY AS RELATED TO OTHER BRANCHES OF SOCIAL SCIENCE.

POLITICAL Economy is closely connected with the other sciences of the same group; those, namely, which deal with philosophy, religion, morality, law, and politics. The object of Political Economy is to determine what laws and what institutions are most favourable to the productivity of labour, and ultimately to the growth and just distribution of wealth.

I have found in the "Encyclopædcia Americana," what I think is a very good definition of Political Economy. "The object of Political Economy is to study the constitution of governments and laws, judicial, social, and financial institutions, education, religion, manners and customs, the soil, the geographical position, climate, the arts, in so far as all these circumstances affect the character and condition of nations relatively to public wealth, that is to the production, distribution, and consumption of all things useful and agreeable in life

Rousseau almost defined it when at the first appearance of the "Contrat Social," he said: " I wish to discover if there can be in the civil order some legitimate and stable system of administration, taking men as they are and laws as they ought to be. I shall endeavour always, in this investigation, to associate the dictates of right with those of interest, so that justice and utility may not be in any degree at variance." The alliance of right with interest, of justice with utility—this is the main and most important point.

It is too often forgotten that this is the light in which the creators of Political Economy, the Physiocrats in France, and Adam Smith in England, regarded the science which they founded. "Political Economy," says the latter, "regarded as a branch of science for statesmen and legislators, has two proper objects: to render the citizens capable of procuring for themselves abundant means of subsistence, and to furnish the government with a revenue proportionate to the public service; in a word, to enrich the people and the sovereign." We have, then, to deal with State laws and not with natural laws.

But, it has been said, it is not then a science at all, it is an art: and it has been proposed to constitute on the one side a science, to deal with general and inevitable laws, and on the other an art, to study the methods of applying these laws. But this is to forget that if we apply the term art to every kind of knowledge which pursues an end, all the moral sciences would deserve this name. Moral Science properly so called does not content itself with describing human passions as they are, it lays down what men ought to do, what duties they should fulfil, and what virtues they ought to practise. Jurisprudence aims at determining what laws ought to be adopted in order that justice may be done. Political science studies what are the forms of government and of institutions that ought to flourish among any given people in order that they may attain the highest degree of civilisation and of prosperity of which they are capable.

The moral sciences have all the same end in view: to lead men up to good, to happiness, to perfection. Need they, therefore, be called arts? I think not. Art begins only when we study the means of winning acceptance for the rules of action which these sciences have discovered.

The economist ought to have in view an ideal:

namely, the well-being of all, in conformity with the prescriptions of what is just. He will then seek out what laws and what institutions lead to this, taking into account human nature in general, and the temperament of each people in particular, and relying on the facts presented to him by history, by statistics, and by the descriptions of different countries he can obtain. He will draw out the relations of cause and effect and deduce from thence practical rules.

Thus an immense horizon opens before us. We are no longer occupied only in stating these so-called natural laws of which we hear so much, and which are nothing but simple truisms, or in analysing with more or less detail the effects of the law of supply and demand, but in studying what are the laws and what the institutions which a society ought to adopt in order to arrive at the highest good.

In this order, a preliminary question presents itself

which brings out the close connection between economic and political science. Which form of government is most favourable to the increase of wealth? This point is not dealt with in manuals, but some writers, among them Montesquieu and Tocqueville, have thrown light upon it. 1 will quote, for instance, such words as these, in the "*Eprit des Lois:*" "Countries are not cultivated by reason of their fertility, but by reason of their liberty." "Despotism is like the savage who cuts down the tree to gather the fruit." I may refer likewise to the following admirable chapters. "How in the democratic state equality is established by laws" (v. 6), and that entitled "Luxury in China," which contains a burning satire on the abuses of the ancient *régime* [1]; again the 13th Book:—"On the relation

---

[1] "'Our ancestors,' said an Emperor of the Tang dynasty, 'considered it a maxim that if there was one man who did no labour, and one woman who altogether failed to spin, then there was someone in the empire who suffered from hunger and cold,'

which the levying of taxes and the greatness of public revenues bear to liberty;" the 18th, "On laws in connection with the nature of the soil;" the 20th, "On laws in relation to commerce," and, finally, the whole book which deals with population.

Rousseau again puts forth here and there very profound views on this subject, as when he shows by the examples of Greece, Rome, and the Italian Republics that the agitations produced by liberty are less fatal than the repose of despotism. "Riots and civil wars are formidable enough to those in authority; but it is not they which cause the real unhappiness of the people." Their true prosperity or calamity springs out of their permanent conditions. When all are crushed under the yoke, then everything droops and

and on this principle he caused an immense number of monasteries of bonzes to be destroyed. So many men being occupied in making the clothes for one, how in the world can there fail to be many who lack clothing? There are ten men to consume the revenue to one who labours to produce it : how in the world can there fail to be numbers who lack nourishment?"

withers, and their rulers destroy them at their ease— "*ubi solitudinem faciunt pacem apellant*"—they have made a desert, and call it peace. Greece was vigorous and flourishing of old, in spite of the most cruel wars; blood flowed in torrents, and, nevertheless, the fields were covered with men.

" It seemed," said Machiavelli, " that in the midst of murders, proscriptions, civil wars, our republic became but the more powerful : the virtue of its citizens, their manners, their independence, had more effect in strengthening than all its dissensions in weakening it. A little agitation gives a spring to the mind, and it is less to peace than to liberty that the race owes what prosperity it has." This is an instance of how history throws light on economic problems.

Rousseau makes another remark which is strikingly true: "Our laws ought to be such that as a means of acquiring abundance, labour should

·be always necessary and never useless." And again, a saying which constantly occurred to my mind when I was travelling recently in Russia : "At each palace which I see rise in the capital, in my mind's eye I seem to see a whole country-side reduced to ruins."

If anyone wishes to have an idea of the effect of bad government let him read the history of the decay of Spain from Philip II. onwards, or let him cross the deserted plains, the bare hill-sides, the fever-stricken valleys of Asia Minor, and think of the wealthy cities and the immense populations which in the olden days inhabited that beautiful country.

Tocqueville has drawn a never-to-be-forgotten picture of the influence of democracy in the pursuit of wealth. "All the causes that nourish in the human heart the love of the good things of this world develope commerce and industry.

Equality is one of these causes. It favours commerce, not directly in giving men a taste for business, but indirectly in strengthening and universalising in men's minds the desire for well-being." "I do not know," he says again, "if one could name a single commercial and manufacturing people, from the Tyrians down to the Florentines and the English, which has not been a free people. There is therefore a close relation and necessary connection between these two things, liberty and industry."

How clearly he points out the danger involved, even from a purely economic point of view, in seeking salvation from absolute power! "Men who have a passion for material enjoyment usually discover how much the agitations produced by liberty disturb their prosperity long before they perceive how liberty itself serves to ensure it, and when the least sound of popular passion penetrates the petty pleasures of their private life, they are aroused and disquieted at once; for a long time the fear of anarchy keeps them incessantly in suspense, and always ready to part with their liberty at the first symptoms of disorder. A nation which expects from its government nothing but the maintenance of order is already, in its heart, a slave: it is the slave of its own prosperity, and at any moment the man may appear who will actually place it in chains." Here we have the events of 1852 predicted long beforehand.

The same writer shows also great insight and observation in the chapters in which he describes the characteristics of modern industry, and the relations between employer and employed which result therefrom.

In Dupont White's clever and thoughtful works we see again at every page the close connection between Economics and Politics.

Another chapter might be written, and would contain more than one piquant and instructive paragraph, on the influence exerted by different forms of worship on the productivity of labour and the prosperity of nations. What renders labour productive is the application of science to industry, and the maintenance of justice in laws. Every religion, then, which condemns the study of nature, or which consecrates deep-seated iniquities or great absurdities, would prove an obstacle to economic progress. The ancient religion of China, and the creed of Zoroaster, both placed agriculture and the planting of trees in the rank of acts of piety. Hence the great prosperity of China and Persia afterwards, while to this day the Parsees in India are almost all very rich, and the Chinese make their fortunes everywhere.

The Mosaic creed proved also very conducive to the progress of economic well-being. It transformed the barren rocks of Palestine into an extremely flourishing and fertile country, with an abundant food supply, and ten times richer and more populous than the Palestine of our time. Before our eyes to-day, the followers of Moses become everywhere the kings of commerce and of finance. In some countries, such as those of Eastern Europe, where the population has not yet wholly recovered from the effects of oppression, as soon as the way is open to free competition, the Jews carry the day so triumphantly against all comers that exceptional measures are passed to handicap them, and sometimes they are even massacred, as in Russia.

Mahomedanism has been the ruin of all countries where it has reigned supreme, with the exception of Egypt, which, thanks to the beneficent Nile, it could not altogether devastate. Its dogmas differed but little from those of Judaism; but it established despotism, disdained science, and inculcated a habit of fatalistic indifference this was quite sufficient to sterilize everything. The cult which began by burning the library of Alexandria could not be favourable to the advance of enlightenment, nor, consequently, to the accumulation of wealth.[1]

Christianity, by preparing the way for the enfranchisement of all mankind, and by introducing everywhere ideas of equality and justice, brought about the magnificent expansion of modern civilisation. To be convinced of this we have only to compare the powerful position of the Christian States with those of other countries, and to note that the freest and most prosperous peoples are precisely those which by religious reform have approached most nearly to the principles of the Gospel. More than this, the sects which have applied these principles in almost all their strictness—the Quakers in England and America, the Mennonites in Holland and Germany, have no paupers, and almost all their members are in easy or opulent circumstances. A Quaker lives exactly as

[1] See my book on the Balkan Peninsula, II. Ch. 6.

Jesus would have men live, and as Political Economy to-day advises. He works steadily and with ardour; he is sober; he avoids luxury in his clothing and in his house; he helps his fellow-men, and at the same time he saves; he thus fructifies industry, creates capital, and lays the foundations of liberty. It is the spirit of the Pilgrim Fathers to which is due the astonishing development of the United States.

CHAPTER II.

POLITICAL ECONOMY AS RELATED TO MORALITY.

QUESTIONS of morality lie at the very roots of Political Economy. For of what, in fact, does its subject-matter consist? The accumulation of wealth. But what is wealth? It is, as Roscher justly says, everything which satisfies a true human need—a need, that is, worthy of human nature and recognised by human reason; in a word a rational need.

Now, who is to say what are rational needs? It is for hygiene to determine what are the real requirements of the body, and it is for morality to prescribe within what limits it is right to give them satisfaction. The moral law condemns on the one hand the asceticism which canonises Simon Stylites for living perched on the summit of a column, or Saint Labre for living in dirt and idleness; and, on the other hand, the Sybarite who awakens amid the scent of rose leaves and whom the service of a thousand domestics cannot satisfy

It is not right to so abuse and mortify the body that it can no longer be the instrument of the mind, but neither is it right to soften and enervate it so that it keeps us incessantly occupied with its fancies. The Greeks, as I said before, may serve us as models in this respect. They took much thought for the body, but only to fortify and invigorate it so that it might be insensible of fatigue, proof against the weather, and almost beyond the reach of disease. At the same time, they carried on the cultivation of the mind by discussions on philosophy and politics, and by the pursuit of art considered as a means of education.

Moral teaching at all times has preached moderation of desires. On the other hand, most economists

regard it as a cause for congratulation that the desires of man are unlimited : because thus, however
rapid progress machinery may make, there will
always be as much work to be done. Of these con-
flicting doctrines, which is the right one ? Evidently
that held by the moralists. If machinery shortens
the time necessary for affording satisfaction to
rational wants, are we to use this leisure which
science has won for us in manufacturing useless
trifles, solely to make work ? This is what Bastiat
calls "sisyphism," that is, making work for work's
sake, digging holes in order to fill them up, pouring
water into the Danaid's cask; and yet Bastiat de-
clared this sisyphism to be necessary for solving the
problem of machinery. Shall we invent childish
fancies, for no reason but to give employment to
workmen ? A sensible man, having once by perfecting his processes of work arrived at procuring
what he requires in a day's work of eight hours, will

not surely devote the rest of his day to embroidering his cuffs or carving himself trinkets. Like the Athenian citizen he will put on a garment of wool and go to hear Socrates lecture, to applaud a play of Sophocles, or to carry on a discussion with Demosthenes. It is thus that the human race should employ itself. See the shops in our large towns : what lost labour does this innumerable variety of useless objects represent, and how much better it would have been to have devoted it to the manufacture of necessaries ! The supreme utility of machinery is not to allow of the indefinite development of luxury, but to assure to everyone the necessaries of life, and to leave men leisure for cultivation of their minds, for the enjoyment of nature and of the society of their fellowmen. *Our material wants are the chains which enslave us.* To satisfy them requires a sacrifice of time, the precious and too scanty material of which our lives are made. He who becomes their slave renounces liberty to devote himself in peace to the pleasures of an idle life.

Economists have been wrong to disregard on this point the words of moralists, both pagan and Christians. *True economic science is in complete agreement with true morality.*

It is the moralist again who must deal with this fundamental question: is everything wealth which has an exchangeable value ? Dupont de Nemours, the latest of the Physiocrats, exiled from France at the Restoration, wrote on the 22nd of April, 1815, from the vessel which was carrying him to America to J. B. Say, reproaching him for having confined the domain of Political Economy within too narrow limits. "It is," he maintains, "the science of justice applied to all social relations. You hold that everything that can be exchanged is wealth. Laïs and Phryne take in exchange for their favours large sums of money: must we conclude from this that they are wealth-producers, and that a country is prosperous in proportion to the number of girls it contains who make money by their charms?   No," he adds truly, "good women are the nation's true treasures, whose price is in inverse proportion to their passing from hand to hand."

An author writes an immoral book, which sells to a hundred editions and brings him in £2000.   Those who buy it are worth less than they were before they read it: they will fulfil their duties less efficiently. Is this book, whose sale has brought such enormous profits to publisher and author, a form of wealth?

The English sell the Chinese 12 millions worth of opium yearly: is that really wealth?   Clearly not. As a matter of fact, if the Emperor had all this opium flung into the sea, so far from China's losing by it, she would gain immensely by having fewer of her people brutalised and incapable of working.   Can that be called wealth the loss of which enriches?

Opium has a value for the merchant, when he finds people foolish enough to give him in exchange for it the money which will procure him useful commodities. But for the nation and for the race it has no value, since it serves only to produce stupefaction and idiocy. It is the same in a less degree with tobacco and strong liquors. These are poisons produced at the cost of labour and capable of exchange, hence, according to the economists, they are forms of wealth—and yet their complete destruction would be a benefit to mankind. We must then distinguish between true and false wealth, and it is to morals and hygiene that we must look to make this important distinction.

The influence of the moralist is felt at every step in dealing with economic questions. The basis of credit is confidence, and confidence rests on the security of honesty and of good laws. Where commercial good faith is lacking, credit cannot exist, or the rate of interest will be exorbitant. There would be an end of industry if there were never a cashier but drained the contents of the cash-box, not a treasurer but manipulated his accounts, not a director but made false balance-sheets in order to dispose of his shares, not a promoter of enterprise but applied for starting companies that he might rob the public. We do not expect to see commodities multiply and commerce flourish in a Forest of Bondy; and it is not hard to discover why the East is not like England. Countries where there is no honesty among officials suffer severely from this cause. Russia and Turkey afford every day sad examples of this.

Moral forces act powerfully on the productivity of labour. The workman who, as the saying is, has his heart in his work, and who fulfils his task from a sense of duty, or even of self-respect, will do by far the best work. He would not do half the amount, of course, if he thought of only applying the famous rule of self-interest, which consists in giving the least possible quantity at the highest possible price.

How important, again, is commercial honesty in the delivery of goods! The salesman who deceives his customers, especially those in foreign countries, closes this opening not only for himself but also for the country to which he belongs.

The landlord who does not press his tenants too hard, but helps them when they are in trouble, and thus establishes kindly relations between himself and them, averts that hostility between class and class which is the peril of the future.

The well-known population question, which in Political Economy overshadows all others, must be solved mainly by considerations which belong to the domain of morals. What is wanted to ensure that the number of inhabitants shall not outstrip the available food supply? Foresight, prudence, and self-restraint alone are wanted, and these are all virtues which presuppose moral force.

The creation of capital is often a virtuous act, especially on the part of people in modest circumstances. It involves the renunciation of an immediate enjoyment for the sake of a future good; and this again requires moral force. As for consumption in general, which, as we have seen, ultimately gives the cue to production, it is determined entirely by the more or less moral direction which is given to life. It is through a decline of morals that a people comes to spend on strong drink an amount sufficient to set it entirely free from misery and want, and it is from the same cause that the rich set the example of prodigality and disorderly living.

The ancients, and even Montesquieu, believed that the increase of wealth leads nations inevitably into effeminacy and decay. This is how they explain the downfall of empires. It is true that if a people, on emerging from primitive simplicity, grows rapidly rich without at the same time acquiring the necessary moral force to enable it to make a good use of its wealth, then this latter will become a source of immorality and the cause of its ruin. This it is which we see going on to-day in the United States. Democracies have always been ruined by excessive inequality rather than by excess of wealth. But a whole book would be necessary to deal fully with such considerations as these.

CHAPTER III.

POLITICAL ECONOMY AS RELATED TO LAW.

WITHOUT Political Economy it is impossible to go at the root of law, just as without the study of law one cannot go at the root of Political Economy. The best jurists are those who are also economists, and the best economists those who are also jurists. But this fact has not been fully recognised by either side, and hence both are often superficial.

The old school of economic science paid almost no attention whatever to questions of law. It conceived of man as acting in complete liberty, following economic laws that were everywhere necessary and everywhere the same. In this region of abstraction there was no need to consider civil institutions and established laws. All that was required was the entire abolition of State interference, by which was understood only the abolition of certain restrictions on individual liberty, such as customs, guild-master-ships and laws against usury. It was altogether forgotten that the State also intervenes in imposing certain forms of property and of inheritance, in a word, the whole civil code, and that, consequently, to call for the absolute suppression of State intervention was to ask for a return to the savage state.

It was thought that the so-called natural laws of Political Economy were the same for all nations and for all countries. "Political Economy," said one of the late Chancellors of the Exchequer, Mr. Lowe, " does not belong to any people in particular. It is founded on the characteristic attributes of human nature, and no power can change it." These are pure abstractions. It is true that no legislator can change the human body or its faculties, can give a man four arms or root out his love of self. ·But he can teach him to regulate his egoism by inspiring him with an enthusiasm for justice, charity, and progress. Further, if the law keeps three parts of the population in slavery, as at Athens or at Rome, economic laws will have a quite different effect from what they have in countries where liberty reigns. And again the distribution of wealth in a country where entail is by law established will differ widely from that in a country under the system of equal partition.

In all societies, except, perhaps, where primitive barbarism lingers, a man's liberty has play only within the limits imposed by judicial institutions and government regulations. The student who is not content with mere vague and abstract theories will find it necessary first to study the influence of these laws and of these institutions. They are not the same in different countries and at different times, and they modify profoundly the system of production, and still more the distribution of wealth. Thus Sir Henry Maine tells us that in Central India the well-known law of supply and demand almost entirely fails to apply, since everything is regulated by custom. The distribution of the products of the soil is very differently carried out, according as the system of land-tenure in a country is that of metayage (or petty farming on half profits) or of leasehold, hereditary or otherwise; that of small or large properties; that of communal ownership or private ownership. Different forms of inheritance produce essentially different and corresponding modifications in the economic system; as, for instance, in France, democratising the possession of land; in England, on the contrary, concentrating it in the hands of a few great families. Wages will be much more variable in a country where the workmen are crowded into large industrial centres, where they must at any price sell their labour, than in a country where the artisans are scattered, as in Switzerland, over the fields and plains and can thus supplement their resources by the cultivation of their little plot of land.

Can we speak of money without asking, what silver and gold coins does the law allow to be universally received as payment, and to cancel every debt? If we study credit, we cannot fail to take account of the laws which concern banking, lending at interest, bankruptcies and trading companies. The relations of men and things, and of men among themselves are evidently determined by law. Political Economy must therefore necessary assimilate the philosophy and history of law.

These sciences, it is true, ought not to be confused the one with the other, but yet the one cannot be studied without the other. It is impossible otherwise to discuss thoroughly the doctrines of Socialism. Socialists have, in fact, maintained that the economic condition of wages is the result of existing institutions, and they demand the reform of the latter, because they are, as they believe, the real cause of misery. If we are to reply to them with anything more than mere vague generalities, we must work back to the subject of civil law, and examine how far they are necessary and useful, and how far they are prejudicial to national prosperity and the well-being of each and all.

We have seen that the civil organisation of a society determines to a very great extent its methods in the production and distribution of wealth, and that consequently a knowledge of law is indispensable to the economist. The knowledge of Political Economy is no less necessary to the legislator who gives his vote to make laws, to the judges who apply them, and to the jurists who interpret them. No doubt when one is content with mere dissertations on the meaning of the text, the special commentaries are all that one needs; but if one wishes to trace back the enactments of law to their source, there are in many cases economic reasons which supply the key to difficulties of interpretation. I shall prove this by passing rapidly in review the principal divisions of the code, beginning with that of property, which lie at the base of all social order.

Why do we allow to certain persons, under the name of property, the exclusive right to dispose of certain things? Those who hold the theory of natural rights will say it is because this right is the *sine quâ non* of man's individual development and of his liberty. He must have a domain in which he can act as master, otherwise he is a slave. Property is the external sphere of liberty; it is therefore a natural right. This theory is incomplete if it is not based on Political Economy, and, in any case, it appears too absolute. It is only because man has wants to satisfy that he needs to have certain things at his own exclusive disposal. What good would the distinction between mine and thine be to the angels? Would you say that if men, like the early Christians, animated by a profound religious sentiment, should hold everything in common, they should cease to be free? Is not rather the most perfect liberty to be found in the most absolute detachment from worldly interests? Further, would it not appear to be sufficient to apply this exclusive right only to objects of consumption produced by personal activity? Is it necessary to extend it to the soil, to capital, to the very instruments of production? Clearly this cannot be decided on *à priori* grounds. We must bring in economic considerations in order to solve the question. Workmen, farmers, even directors and managers, all work by means of capital, and on land which does not belong to them: are they by this means deprived of " the external sphere of their personal liberty?" If property is the *sine quâ non* of liberty, how comes it that so many millions of men have none? We see, therefore, that natural right without Political Economy will not suffice to give us a solid basis for property.

According to the theory of Roman law, which has been taken up by modern Jurists, property is derived from occupation. He who assumed control over an object which hitherto belonged to no one, *res nullius*, acquires the power of disposing of it to the exclusion of all others.—This explanation is even less satisfactory than the preceding. For an act to give rise to a right, the act must be legitimate in itself, and it must be, at the same time, just and useful that this act should so give rise to a right. So far from founding the legitimacy of property on occupation, we have first to demonstrate the legitimacy of the occupation in itself. Now this, as above stated, rests on an erroneous hypothesis. There is in reality no such thing as a *res nullius*. Every territory, with all that it contains, before the establishment of private property, belongs to the tribe or nation; this latter may, it is true, determine that the first who encloses a piece of land or takes a piece of game becomes thereby the possessor of it; but in this case, it is the law which creates the property, and if it does so it is from motives of general utility of the economic kind. Is it enough for me to plunge my sword into a field or plant my flag upon a continent in order that I may become the owner thereof? And can I, merely by the exercise of my will, trace the limits of my right? Evidently not. It is in the name of justice, and not from a mere act of appropriation, that the right to dispose of an object is to be vindicated. Thus occupation can be a mode of acquiring property sanctioned by law. It cannot be itself the judicial basis of property.

No, the economists will tell you labour is the true basis of property. Is it not just and expedient that he who creates the value of an object, and he who fertilizes the soil, should become the owner of the one and of the other? Here property is founded on a purely economic basis. We can, of course, take as the ideal to be attained such a system of civil institutions as will ensure to each, out of the sum total of the national produce, a part proportioned to the share he has had in the work of production; but economists have failed to see where their theory would lead. It is this very theory that has furnished the Socialists with their most dangerous weapons. If it is labour which creates value, they say, then the whole product of labour ought to go to the labourer. Labour, you say, is the basis of property. If this is so, then pray explain to us how it comes to pass that in every age and in all countries they who labour have no property, and they who have property do not labour It is clear that the theory of the economists, if it is to be the foundation of the social system of the future, is not that of the system which exists to-day.

There remain to consider the theories of the social contract, and of law. The first supposes that in the beginning men made an agreement that they would substitute private property for common property. This is evidently an imaginary transaction, but, even were it real, it could not serve as a basis for an existing institution. How could civilised societies hold themselves bound by a contract formed by our ancestors while still in a state of savagery? The only thing that is really important is the motive which should lead them to set aside the system of common property. This motive was the consideration that the change would give more individual freedom, more inducement to labour, and, as a result, the better cultivation of the soil. This is, in fact, the reason why, in the course of history and by successive stages of progress, the private ownership of the soil has been gradually substituted for the collective ownership. And this reason is evidently of the economic order.

The theory of the social contract has lost credit, but the theory which derives property from positive law still has many adherents. It is so far evident that it is the law which defines property and which determines its privileges, obligations, limits, and modes of acquisition; but the moral law is not made by the legislator. He can even lay down rules contrary to equity, as in sanctioning slavery. His decisions are legitimate only on condition that they are consistent with justice and with public order. At any given time, for any given people, there is a system, a set of institutions, which is more favourable than any other to the well-being and progress of the individuals and of the society. Laws which approximate to this system are good laws, those which are averse to it are bad laws. This is

RIGHT, or the moral law, that is to say, the right course, the shortest and best path towards perfection. This order or system is evidently not the same for all times and for all peoples. Institutions that are excellent for civilised men would lead savages to their ruin. It is for the wise to discover the right and for the legislator to proclaim it. To pretend that a legislator creates right is as much as to say that man creates truth. If private property is the form most favourable to liberty, and to the well-being of man, it must be established by law. If another form of property would be more advantageous, then it must be adopted. In seeking the true basis of institutions, therefore, it is not enough to point to the laws which create them, we must go back to the reasons which render these laws just and good.

We have now passed rapidly in review the five principal theories concerning the origin of property.

They all, in whatever of truth they contain, rest ultimately on considerations which belong to the economic order. At bottom, the motives which justify private property are very simple. In the first place, it is just to recompense an individual for his trouble and his sacrifices by allowing him the fruits of his toil. In the second place, to give a person the entire disposal of the objects produced by him, and even of a portion of the soil, is the best means of inducing him to produce the greatest possible amount, and hence, to better his own condition and to contribute his share to the national wealth. It is, therefore, economic utility which is the true basis of property, and this it is which determines what shall be its privileges, obligations and limits. It is for economic reasons also, that rights of property are more or less extensive, according to the different objects to which they refer: being almost absolute in relation to objects which are moveables, but already limited when we come to arable land; still more restricted for houses and forests, and finally, for mines and railways closely hedged in by the intervention of public authority.

The true foundation of property is very clearly brought out by the reasons which are alleged for establishing this new right which has been called that of *intellectual property*, the right of the author, inventor, patentee, trade marks, and limited companies. There are two motives which prompt this novelty: one of justice, and one of utility. It is just that the composer of a book or work of art, the inventor of an industrial process, the founder of a business firm, should have some recompense for his merit and for his efforts. And further, this is the best means of multiplying good books and pictures, and of encouraging useful inventions by which the whole society will profit. It has been thought well to limit the duration of rights, because a monopoly for a certain number of years seemed enough to stimulate genius, and after that it seemed better that all should be able to profit by the idea, without paying tribute to the descendants of the one who first conceived it. This was thought to be the best means of harmonising public and private interests. Experience alone, that is the observation of the results attained, can decide how far this plan has been successful. It is the same with every other form of property. Not by philosophical deductions, but by a study of facts, by the light of history and statistics, can it be determined what restrictions it is right to impose on private property, having regard to the objects to which it applies.

Let us take some more detailed instances: why were servitudes established? For economic reasons. It is expedient that I should have an outlet for my water, or use the party-wall for the support of my beams. It may not suit you that I should do so,

L

but from considerations of general interest the law allows it me. My estate is enclosed within yours: it is expedient that I should be able to cultivate it: you will have to allow me a right of way through yours.

In the matter of prescription we can see clearly how rights give way before economic interest. A right is in its nature perpetual; it ought not, therefore, to be extinguished by the lapse of time. Nevertheless, Roman law, and modern law following its steps, laid down that whoever occupies an estate 10 or 20 years in good faith and by just title acquires a right of property in it, even against the will, and perhaps without the fault of the real owner. Why have we this deflection from the strictness of judicial principles? Hear what the jurists reply; they call in economic considerations in support of it: He who gives additional value to a holding, who keeps it up, who improves it, incorporates with it, as it were, a part of himself. It is like an outcome and an extension of his own person. This argument contains the whole theory of the economists. Furthermore, property cannot remain long in suspense without injury to the public interest. Troplong, in his well-known "Treatise on Prescription," sets forth these considerations in a manner worthy of Adam Smith or J. B. Say. It is Political Economy which ultimately decides these questions.

After property, the system of inheritance has most influence on the distribution of wealth. Free contract, upon which the economists base everything, does not come into play until each man's share has been decided by the laws of succession and bequest. On what are these laws founded? Not on natural rights, the jurists say. Heirs, even when they are children, have no absolute right to the inheritance, since they can be entirely shut out from it. On the other hand, the presumed or even the expressed wish of the deceased is not law, since many codes lay restrictions on him. It is economic interest again which has served as the basis for various systems of inheritance. At Rome, a man's will decides the reversion of his goods: the last testament is sovereign: *uti legasset ita Jus esto.* Among the Germanic tribes, as among the Slavs and in primitive times generally, there was no will. The children were, so to speak, co-proprietors, or rather the estates were the possession of the family regarded in the eye of the law as a perpetual entity; successive generations had only a life interest in them. Among the Germanic tribes, as in Great Russia to-day, heredity came into play only with regard to the furniture, the house, and the small adjoining enclosure. The possession of land was temporary, and for life only.

Why has heredity been established? Not certainly from the motive of justice. According to modern ideas, merit and demerit cannot be handed down. We no longer admit that "the curse of the Almighty descends from generation to generation." My father occupied a high position because he was worthy of it; that is no reason why it should afterwards pass to me. In the same way, if he had committed a crime, it would not be just to make me bear the penalty. Responsibility is a personal matter; every one should be treated according to his personal merit or demerit. The lazy ought always to suffer the immediate consequences of his idleness, and the laborious man to enjoy the fruits of his work. The considerations which have led to the establishment of heredity and the causes which have guided the history of its development were exclusively economic. If the father has no certainty that the fruits of his toil, and still more of his savings, will pass to his children, he will display far less activity, and he will consume at once all that he produces. Production will thus be less, and the formation of capital *nil*. Inheritance is therefore useful as a stimulus to the accumulation of wealth. To what degree ought collateral successions to extend? Evidently, not beyond the degree at which they can act as an encouragement to work and saving; carried further, they will be nothing but a source of law-suits. It is for this reason that many jurists propose to limit them to the fifth or sixth degree.

Should the father of a family be free to dispose of the whole of his fortune after his death, or should a reserve be established in favour of his children? Most economists are in favour of absolute testamentary freedom. M. Le Play, with a wealth of arguments and facts which has carried conviction to many, makes out that the enforced reserve is one of the chief causes of social disorganisation on the Continent. This fatal clause, he says, ruins paternal authority, destroys the continuity of industrial enterprises, induces the minute sub-division of land, and causes a crowd of other evils to arise. The authors of the French Civil Code aimed at furthering the progress of equality, and of placing property in the hands of the largest possible number. For this reason they abolished entail, substitution, and the absolute freedom of bequest. Who judged rightly, the authors of the Civil Code, or M. Le Play? This is a difficult question to answer, and has to be regarded on many different sides. I cannot even attempt to deal with it here. All I wish to prove is that in order to discover which of the two systems is the best, we must turn to economic considerations, and examine which of the two is most conducive to public prosperity.[1]

---

[1] The arguments on both sides of this question have been well summed up by M. V. Thiry, Rector of the University of Liège (*On Reserve and Freedom of Bequest*). M. Thiry, who pronounces in favour of reserve, brings out clearly the economic aspect of the question. "Of all the civil laws relating to goods," he says, "none are of more importance than those which

Let us examine now the other branches of the Civil Code, the guardianship of minors, the marriage contract and its various regulations, legal and conventional communities, the institution of the dowry, the contracts of sale and hire, privileges and hypothecations, and throughout them all it will be seen that what the legislator has had in view was the preservation, the good administration, and the easy transfer of wealth. And this is precisely the object of political economy. The aim of the different social sciences is the same: to carry man to the highest pitch of perfection which he is capable of attaining. Only each one deals with the things that are in its proper domain. The science of law determines the

regulate the patrimony we leave behind us. On these laws depend not only the just distribution of the wealth of the deceased, as well as the more or less active creation of new wealth by its means; but also, they exert a powerful influence on the constitution of the family, on the inter-relations of its members, and on the harmony and affection which ought to prevail among them, and through this channel, on public order generally."

relations of men to things and to each other. Political Economy, studying the effects of actual laws, dictates to law-makers the rules they ought to lay down.

Commerce and industry, in proportion as they develop, occupy an ever larger place in modern law. The branches which deal with them acquire more importance every day. The attention of the bar is most frequently called to matters having reference to mines, railways, factories, great enterprises of all kinds for employing the capital of the nation. Joint-stock companies, bankruptcies, regulation of accounts, responsibility in matters of transport, give rise every day to disputes of the greatest importance. The wealth represented by titles of all kinds already far exceeds the amount of property in land, and thus law-suits concerning the former kind deal with much more extensive interests than those which relate to landed property. Is it not therefore indispensable for a rising barrister to be thoroughly conversant with Political Economy in order that he may deal with all these essentially economic questions?

CHAPTER IV.

POLITICAL ECONOMY AS RELATED TO HISTORY.

I HAVE a few remarks to make in conclusion. The jurist cannot ignore the leading facts of history, since law, as is more and more admitted, is of historic growth. Now, in tracing back the causes which produced the rise and fall of nations, we find them to be always economic. This is very easily accounted for. Is not the power of empires founded on the growth of population and of wealth, and when these once begin to diminish, is not decay the inevitable result?

Western civilisation began in Egypt, where the people had their riches brought to their feet, as it were, ready-made, by the Nile. Their prosperity,

thus favoured by heaven, held its own against all re-
verses, because it was the work of nature and not of
man. The Greek republics all succumbed under the
pressure of the social difficulty, which harasses and
threatens modern society to-day. In early days,
when everything was at a low level, all the citizens
had some little property, and the legislators tried, by
a great variety of expedients, which Aristotle enume-
rates, to maintain equality of conditions. In the
presence of slavery, a free man could not or would
not live by his own labour, and thus when he had
no other possession left him but his arms, he became a menace to the existing order. In proportion
as the rich absorbed more of the national wealth,
the proletariat increased in numbers. Hence the
struggle between rich and poor, which broke out, not
all at once, but successively in all parts. After a
series of revolutions and counter revolutions, and successive periods of anarchy and despotism, which

alternately engendered each other, this struggle brought about the loss of liberty and of prosperity, and finally resulted in the ruin of the State.

The history of the Roman Empire teaches us a like lesson. At first we see Italy scattered over with small republics; their peasants free, industrious, and equal, all bearing the sword, cultivating each a little domain, and keeping up large flocks and herds on the common pastures. These republics were similar in all respects to the primitive cantons of Switzerland. Rome herself was one of these at the first. She was already powerful at a time when her great men still drove the plough with their own hands. But the constant wars she waged were the ruin of the plebeians. The patricians would encroach on the common lands, the *ager publicus* which was always being enlarged by the confiscation of vanquished territory. War furnished them with slaves to work them. Thus the "*latifundia*" were formed. Tiberius Gracchus, returning from Spain across Italy, beheld nothing but deserted plains everywhere. The free man has disappeared; cultivation has ceased; there remain nothing but immense pastures over which wander herds of cattle and slaves. Gracchus sees the cause of the evil. He desires to do what has been done by the French Revolution, to multiply small proprietorships by an equitable division of the *ager publicus.* But neither his agrarian laws, nor those of Licinius, and a score of other Tribunes of the Plebs, nor yet the distributing of lands made by victorious generals, had power to arrest the advancing progress of large properties, and the destruction of freemen. Inequality goes on increasing. The rich and powerful enrich themselves still further out of the spoils of provinces—the trial of Verres shows us by what means. The number of poor goes on increasing. When the republic has become the prey of a few oligarchs who dispute the supremacy among themselves, then she is ripe for a despotism. Although from time to time power may fall into the hands of good men, the empire, on the whole, only accelerates the causes that are leading to social disorganisation. The depopulation spreads from Italy to the provinces. When the barbarians swarm in, they occupy by degrees the vacant spaces. The *latifundia* and slavery have been the ruin of everything.

In the whole of modern history there is no more striking fact than the rapid fall of Spain from the 16th century onwards. Up to the time of Charles V. she is populous, rich, very well cultivated, enjoying a greater measure of local independence than any other people, full of prosperous industries of all kinds—leather work at Cordova, arms at Toledo, stuffs at Segovia, silks at Seville, felts at Valencia. By a series of political crimes and economic mistakes, the Jews, banks and commerce, the Moors, agriculture, are one by one exterminated; labour is subjected to fines; industry handicapped by senseless taxation; activity and initiative killed by despotism and theocracy; every one ruined by imposts. The fountain of wealth dries up; the population melts away; farms are abandoned; the *despoplados* or desert spreads its confines. Like Italy, after the time of the Gracchi, Castille becomes a great pasture land for the sheep of the *mestra.* Even the Court itself is reduced to misery. Only the convents are rich and populous. In less than a hundred years, Spain, which once made Europe tremble, is reduced to be no more than a State of the third rank. During this time, liberty and commerce are founding the greatness, first of Holland and then of England, who rule by turns upon the ocean. Here, again, we have the effects of economic causes.

In M. Taine's fine book on "*The Origins of Contemporary France*" there is a chapter which ought to be read in this connection, on the fearful misery of France under the old *régime.* It is a companion picture to that of Spain under the descendants of Philip II. Here again the land lies waste, the most industrious citizens are proscribed by intolerance, marriages are sterile, population diminishes, misery becomes general. Despotism here as elsewhere accom plishes its accursed work of ruin and desolation.

How has it come about that the German Empire has passed from the hands of Austria into those of Prussia? A Hohenzolleran, petty Margrave of Nuremberg, and very economical, lends some money to the magnificent Emperor Sigismund, who is very lavish. The latter, not being able to pay his creditor. either interest or capital, hands over to him in pay- ment the March of Brandenburg. Out of this grows Prussia, who among her arid sands has made her way by economy. Frederic II., type of his race, formed the nation on his own model: having no personal wants,

M

he devotes all his means to the State. He improves the breed of horses, founds model farms, builds schools, makes roads and dikes, and thus, notwithstanding some disastrous wars, enriches his country, while Louis XIV. and XV. were ruining theirs. On the fateful day of Sadowa, modest Prussia stood supplied with the most perfect instruments of war, because she had known how to manage her limited resources with the strictest economy, and by this means she conquered Austria, a country much more wealthy, much more powerful, but always badly administered.

See again what is happening in the East. In the last war between Russia and Turkey (1877), the latter succumbed in spite of the bravery of her soldiers, less by the victories of her enemies than by her own economic incompetence. The Turks have reduced to barrenness every country they occupy; they have never taken any measures to encourage labour. They have even allowed roads and bridges to fall into ruins which were made before their time. They have no knowledge of how to create capital, and by their detestable system of imposts they hinder others from accumulating it. Thus the Ottoman empire, attacked by an incurable economic malady, has declined steadily. It has lost its provinces one by one. Its boundaries have shrunk. Its population has diminished. The revenues squandered, the treasury empty, bankruptcy ensues, and proves the destruction of credit. The introduction of railways, the working of mines, and the larger forms of industry would scarcely better the condition of the Turks, for these works would bring profit chiefly to the Christians, who would thus become their masters.

Thus it has been clearly shown that economic causes are at work in producing the rise and fall of empires.

THE END.

BIBLIOGRAPHY OF THE AUTHOR'S WORKS.

Extracts from the *Bibliographie Academique* (1886 edition).

ÉMILE DE LAVELEYE, O., living at Liège, born at Bruges in 1822; docteur en droit; professeur d'économie politique et d'économie industrielle à l'Université de Liège, membre de l'Académie royale de Belgique, correspondant de l'Institut de France, des Lincei de Rome, des Académies royales de Lisbonne, de Madrid, de Belgrade, etc. Dr. Honoris causâ of Edinburgh, Würzburg, etc.

WORKS PUBLISHED BY THE ACADÉMIE ROYALE DE BELGIQUE.

Rapport sur les mémoires de concours de 1869 relatifs à une description statistique d'une commune des Flandres.

Rapport sur les mémoires de concours de 1872 relatifs à la théorie économique du capital et du travail.

Rapport sur les mémoires do concours de 1874 relatifs au même sujet.

Du respect de la propriété privée sur mer en temps de guerre, lecture faite en séance publique de la Classe des lettres le 16 ma, 1877.

La démocratie et l'économie politique, discours prononcé comme directeur de la Classe des lettres en séance publique du 8 mai 1878. —Ce discours a été publié aussi eu allemand, 8vo. *Eisenach*, 1878.

Rapport sur les mémoires de concours de 1880 relatifs à l'histoire des classes rurales en Belgique jusqu'a la fin du XVIII. siècle

Rapport sur les mémoires de concours de 1881 concernant l'histoire des finances publiques de la Belgique depuis 1830.

Sur divers objets de bronze antique trouvés à Angleur, près de Liège.

Rapport sur les mémoires de concours de 1882 relatifs à l'organisation des institutions charitables en Belgique, et sur les finances publiques de la Belgique depuis 1830.

Notes bibliographiques sur divers ouvrages.

Rapport sur un travail de M.O. Merten : Étude sur François Huet.

Rapport sur le mémoire de concours de 1886, concernant les anciens corps de métiers et les associations coopératives dans les temps modernes.

Notice nécrologique sur H.-G. Moke. Annuaire. Année 1870.

WORKS NOT PUBLISHED BY THE ACADÉMIE
DE BELGIQUE.

Album d'Ostende. Dessins par Louis Ghémar et E. Manche, obl. fol. *Ostende*, 1841.

Histoire de la langue et de la littérature provençales, 347 pp. 8vo. *Brussels*, 1845 ; Mémoire couronné au concours universataire.

Histoire des rois francs, 2 vols. 12mo. *Brussels*, 1847-1848.

L'armée et l'enseignement, 20 pp. 8vo. *Brussels*, 1848.

Le Sénat belge. Étude politique, 68 pp. 8vo. *Brussels*, 1851.

Études historiques et critiques sur le principe et les conséquences de la liberté du commerce international, iv.-146 pp. 8vo. *Brussels*, 1857.

Débats sur l'enseignement primaire dans les Chambres hollandaises (session de 1857), 79 pp. 8vo. *Gand*, 1858.

Du progrès des peuples anglo-saxons, 47 pp. 8vo. *Brussels*, 1859.

De l'enseignement obligatoire, 57 pp. 12mo. *Brussels*, 1859.

La question de l'or en Belgique, 81 pp. 12mo. *Brussels*, 1860.

Les Nibelungen. Traduction nouvelle, précédée d'une étude sur la formation de l'épopée, lxxix.-357 pp. 12mo. *Brussels*, 1861.

Mémoires de Sir Robert Peel. *Brussels*, 1861-1862 ; 2 vols. in-8 ; Traduction de l'anglais.

Questions contemporaines, 353 pp. 12mo. *Brussels*, 1863.

Études d'économie rurale.—La Néerlande ; précédée du rapport de M. Léonce de Lavergne sur l'Économie rurale de la Belgique, xxiii.-360 pp. 12mo. *Brussels*, 1864.

Le marché monétaire depuis cinquante ans. 8vo. Paris, 1865 ; German transl. *sub. lit.* : Die Geld- und Handelskrisen, 8vo. *Cassel*, 1865.

La Saga des Nibelungen dans les Eddas et dans le Nord scandinave. Traduction précédée d'une étude sur la formation des épopées nationales, 390 pp. 12mo. *Brussels*, 1866.

L'Edda. Traduction des poèmes scandinaves, 12mo. *Brussels*, 1866.

La Lombardie et la Suisse. Étude d'économie rurale, 12mo. Paris, 1869 ; Portugese, transl. *sub. lit.* : A Lombardia, a Suissa e o monte Rosa (D'Venacio Deslandes), 178 pp. 8vo. Lisboa, 1871.

La question du grec et la réforme de l'enseignement moyen.—
—Quelques pièces du procès, recueillies et mises en ordre, 138 pp. 8vo. *Brussels*, 1869.

Études et essais, 12mo. *Paris*, 1869.

La Prusse et l'Autriche depuis Sadowa, 2 vols. 12mo. Paris, 1870. (Articles publiés dans la *Revue des Deux Mondes*.)

Idem ; German transl. *sub. lit.*: Die œsterreich-ungarische Monarchie nach dem Kriege von 1866. *Pest*, 1869.

Essai sur les formes de gouvernement dans les sociétés modernes,

192 pp. 12mo. *Paris*, 1872. Extrait de la *Revue des Deux Mondes.*
—Italian transl. in *Bibliotheca di Scienzie politiche.*

L'instruction du peuple, 488 pp. 8vo. *Paris*, 1872; two Dutch transls., one Swedish *sub. lit.* : Vär Tids Folksundervisning, ofversatt och försedt met eft tillägg röraude Folkskoleväsendets nuvarande ställning inom de trenne Skandinaviska Länderna, af Hugo Hamilton, 119 pp. 12mo. *Stockholm*, 1872.

Des causes actuelles de guerre en Europe et de l'arbitrage, 8vo. *Brussels*, 1863; English transl.

Rapport sur le prix Guinard. L'épargne dans l'école. *Brussels*, 1873.

Le parti clérical en Belgique. Avers, 60 pp. 4to., 1873; 111 pp. 12mo. *Brussels*, 1874; English and Dutch transls.

Une leçon de droit public à l'Université de Louvain, 8vo. *Brussels*, 1874.

De la propriété de ses formes primitives, 395 pp. 8vo. *Paris*, 1874. Five editions. English, German, Danish and Russian transls.

Essai sur l'économie rurale de la Belgique, 402 pp. 8vo. *Brussels*, 1862; transls. 2nd edn. 18mo. *Paris*, 1875.

Les actes de la Conférence de Bruxelles et la participation de la Belgique à la Conférence de Saint-Pétersbourg, 35 pp. 8vo. *Brussels*, 1875.

Du respect de la propriété privée en temps de guerre. Rapport présenté à l'Institut de droit international (août 1875, 49 pp. 8vo.) *Brussels*, 1875; German transl.

Il congresso dei socialisti della Cattedra ad Eisenach. Lettera al direttore del *Giornale degli Économisti*, 20 pp. 8vo. *Padua*, 1875.

Le protestantisme et le catholicisme dans leurs rapports avec la liberté et la prospérité des peuples. Étude d'économie sociale, 39 pp. 8vo. *Brussels*, 1875; 61 pp. 12mo, 1876; English, with introd. by W. E. Gladstone; German, Dutch, Portugese, Swedish, Hungarian, Modern-Greek, Polish, Italian, Spanish, Chech transls.

De l'avenir des peuples catholiques. Étude d'économie sociale, 8vo. *Paris*, 1875. (Reprint of the above work.)

La monnaie bimétallique, 8vo. *Brussels*, 1876; English and German transls.

L'avenir religieux des peuples civilisés, 30 pp. 8vo. *Brussels*, 1876; German, Spanish, Portugese, Swedish and Modern-Greek transls.

L'Afrique centrale et la Conférence géographique de Bruxelles, 87 pp. 18mo. *Brussels*, 1877.

L'Afrique centrale et la Conférence géographique de Bruxelles. Lettres et découvertes de Stanley, 220 pp. and 2 maps, 18mo. *Brussels*, 1878.

Histoire de la liberté dans l'antiquité et le christianisme, par lord Acton, préface d'Ém. de Laveleye, 93 pp. 12mo. *Brussels*, 1878.

Congrès agricole international de Paris, 1878.—L'agriculture belge.—Rapport présenté au nom des sociétés agricoles de la Belgique, cclxxix.-377 pp. and map, 8vo. *Brussels*, 1878.

Considération sur la constitution belge, introduction à l'histoire du Congrès par Théodore Juste. *Brussels*, 1879.

La crise économique et les chemins de fer vicinaux, 23 pp. 8vo. *Brussels*, 1877.

Lettres d'Italie, 1878-1879, 394 pp. 12mo. *Brussels*, 1880.

Congrès international du commerce et de l'industrie.—La question monétaire.—Section d'économie politique, 15 pp. 8vo. *Brussels*, 1880.

La question monétaire en 1881, 80 pp. 8vo. *Brussels*, 1881.

Le bimétallisme international, 30 pp. *Paris*, 1881; English transl.

Le crédit agricole, 10 pp. 8vo. *Brussels*, 1881.

Le vice patenté, 40 pp. 8vo. *Brussels*, 1882.

Élements d'économie politique, 325 pp. 12mo. *Paris*, 1882; (2 eds.) English, Dutch, Italian, Chech, Polish, Portugese, Serbian, and Bulgarian transls.

Le socialisme contemporain, 1st ed. 8vo. *Brussels*; 2nd et 3rd eds., 333 pp. 12mo. *Paris*. English, German, Swedish, Chech, and Russian transls.

Nouvelles lettres d'Italie, 218 pp. 8vo. *Brussels*, 1884; English transl.

Le vice légalisé, 30 pp. 8vo. *Brussels*, 1884; English transl.

La crise récente en Belgique, 25 pp. *Paris*, 1885; English transl.

La Péninsule des Baldans, 2 vols. 12mo. *Brussels*, 1886; English, German, and Bulgarian transls.

La propriété collective en divers pays, 60 pp. 8vo. *Brussels*, 1886.

La crise et la contraction monétaire, 15 pp. 8vo. *Paris*, 1886; Spanish transl. (*Buenos-Ayres*) and Serbian transl.

La crise et ses remèdes, 100 pp. *Verviers*, 1886.

COLLABORATION.

"La Flandre libérale," *Gand* (1848-1849), "La libre Recherche," "Revue trimestrielle," "Revue britannique," "Revue germanique," "Revue des Deux-Mondes," "Exposition universelle de Paris en 1867," "Jury belge Documents et Rapports," "Moniteur belge," "Revue de Belgique," "Cobden Club Essays," "Revue de Droits international & de législation comparée," "The Fortnightly Review," "Journal de Liège," "L'Indépendance belge," "The Times," "The Daily News," "The Academy," "The Penn Monthly Magazine," "Journal des Économistes," "Giornale degli Economisti," "Nederlandsch Museum," "Patria Belgica," "Rotterdamsche Courant," "La Flandre libérale," *Gand* (1876-1879), "Bankers' Magazine," New York, "Nuova Antologia" (*Rome*), "Der Staats-Socialist" (5th Nov. 1880), "L'Économiste français," "Revue scientifique," "Jahrbücher für national Œkonomie," "Het Volksbelang," "Bibliothèque Gilon."

PRINCIPAL MAGAZINE ARTICLES NON REPRODUCED
IN VOLUME FORM.

Revue des Deux Mondes : Les partis en Belgique, 1 Aug. 1864.—
La monnaie internationale, Apl. 1867.—Le voyage de la Novare, 15
Jan. 1868, (transl. into Portugese).—Deak Ferencz, 15 Aug. 1869,
(transl. into Hungarian). La libertié de l'enseignement supéricur en
Belgique 15 Apl. 1870.—La question agraire en Irlande et en Angleterre, 15 June, 15 July, 1870.—Le régime parlementaire en Italie,
1 May 1871.—La nouvelle politique de la Russie, 15 Nov. 1871.—La
crise récente eu Belgique, 15 Jan. 1872, (transl. into Dutch and
Swedish).—Les Latifundia de l'Agro Romano, 1 June 1872.—Les
progrès de l'enseignement en Russie, 15 Apl. 1874.—Le Gouvernement de la République des Provinces-Unies, 15 Aug. 1874.—Les lois
des Brehons, 15 Apl. 1875.—Les tendances nouvelles de l'économie
politique 15 July 1875, (transl. into English and German).—La production et la consommation actuelle des métaux précieux 1 Aug. 1878.
—Grandeur et décadence de l'Internationale, 15 Mch. 1880, (transl.
into Dutch).—Bakounie, 1 June 1880, (transl. into Hungarian).—La
Russie et l'Angleterre en Orient, 15 July 1880.—Le Luxe, 1 Nov.
1880, (transl. into Portugese in Brazil).—Cliffe Leslie, 15 Aug. 1881,
(transl. into English at New York).—Le président Garfield, 1 Oct.
1881, (transl. into Swedish, Dutch, Portugese, and Spanish).—Le
régime parlementaire et la démocratie, Dec. 1882.—La démocratie
aux États-Unis et en Suisse, 1 Oct. 1886. La transformation du
gouvernement local aux Etats-Unis, 1 Aout, 1889.—Un précurseur,
Dupont, White, 1 Dec. 1889.

Revue de Belgique : De l'utilité du théâtre, Jan. 1869.—La revanche
de la France, Jan. 1872.—Une leçon de droit public à l'Université de
Louvain, Jan. 1874, (as pamphlet 17 pp. 8vo.).—Le double pro-
gramme du parti libéral, Jan. 1877, (as pamphlet 27 pp. 8vo.).—De
la difficulté de fonder la liberté en France, Nov. 1877.—Le sénateur

Reyntiens, Apl. 1879.—La bataille des étalons, May 1881, (transl. into English).—La séparation de l'Église et de l'État, Aug. 1881, (repr. at Paris as preface to the work of M. Minghetti under same title).—L'histoire de l'agriculture en Italie, Jan. 1882, (as pamphlet 21 pp.).—L'Allemagne et l'Italie, Feb. 1882.—La question égyptienne, Aug. 1882, (as pamphlet 25 pp.).—La modernité dans l'art, Oct. 1882. —L'instruction supérieure pour les femmes, 15 Nov. 1882.—L'Association internationale au Congo, Dec. 1882.—La crise du libéralism Dec. 1883, (as pamphlet 30 pp.).—Cinq années de régime constitutionnel en Bulgarie, Oct. 1884.—Lettres inédites de Stuart Mill, Jan. 1885. —Les conditions économiques du Congo, Apl. 1885.—En Roumanie, 15 Jan. (transl. into Roumanian).—Essais de droit public, July 1886.

Fortnightly Review : The future of France, June 1871.—The clerical party in Belgium, Nov. 1872, (transl. into French, Dutch, and German).—Alienation of public lands in Colonies, June 1874.—The European situation, July 1875.—English interests, July 1877.— England and the war, Feb. 1873.—Belgian politics, Aug. 1878.— Bismarck und seine Leute, Dec. 1878.—Italian politics, Apl. 1879. —Austro-German Alliance, Dec. 1879.—Bimetallism and Free trade, July 1881.—Egypt for the Egyptians, Dec. 1882.—European terror, Apl. 1883, (transl. into Danish).—Townships in Scotland, June 1885.

Contemporary Review : Commonplace Fallacies concerning money, Nov. and Dec. 1881.—Politics in Belgium, Apl. 1882.—Progress and Poverty, Nov. 1882.—Progress of Socialism, Apl. 1883.—Congo neutralised, June 1883.—The prospects of the French Republic, Nov. 1883.—The liberal defeat in Belgium and its causes, Aug. 1884.— Würtzburg and Vienna, Nov. and Dec. 1884.—The State versus man, with the reply of Herbert Spencer, Apl. 1885, (repr. in French in the *Revue internationale* of [Florence]) May 1885.—Pessimism on the Stage, Sept. 1885.—The économic crisis and its causes, Mch. 1886 (transl. into Spanish at Buenos-Ayres).—The Situation in the Easth, Nov. 1880. Future of religion, Oct. 1889. Two new Utopias, Jan. 1890. Communism, March 1890.

Nineteenth Century : The future of God, Sept. 1881, (repr. in *Indépendance belge,* Oct. 1881).—Maritime capture, Aug. and Sept. 1882.

Flandre Libérale : (Revue), 1848 : Les lettres de Michel Chevalier. —La critique d'art.—Le parti catholique.—Emploi de l'armée dans les travaux publics.

Express europeen : Les mésaventures d'un parchemin, (transl. into Danish and Swedish).—Chasse à l'ours dans les Karpathes.

Encyclopedia americana : Commercial crisis.

Revue chrétienne : La crise en Belgique, Jan. 1885, (transl. into English in the *Congregationalist,* June 1885).—La démocratie et le protestantisme, July 1886.

Journal des Économistes : La nouvelle école économique, June 1879. —Les lois naturelles et l'économie politique, Apl. 1883, (as pamphlet 22 pp.).—La crise et la contraction monétaire, Mch. 1885, (transl. into Spanish at Buenos-Ayres).

Jahrbücher für national Œkonomie : Régime agraire de l'Oudhe, Aug. 1880.

Revue politique et littéraire : Les troubles en Belgique, 11 Apl. 1886. —Hamlet, 25 Sept. 1886.—Le gouvernement populaire, 1 Dec. 1886.

Nederlandsch museum : Het Darwinism en het Rechtsvaardigheid's begrip, Dec. 1874.

European Correspondance : Church and State in Belgium, 19 Mch. 1887.

La Revue internationale : Le Plébiscite, Feb. 1887.—La reforme du regime parlementaire, Nov. 1888.

The Forum : Civil Government and the Papacy, Ap. 1888.—Perils of Democracy, May 1889.—Mutterings of War, Oct. 1889.

www.ingramcontent.com/pod-product-compliance
Lightning Source LLC
Chambersburg PA
CBHW030552040726
47497CB00008B/2695